Kailin Gow

Beautiful

Girl

Modern Beauty and Beast

kailin gow

A Contemporary Adult Novel

Beautiful Girl: Modern Beauty and Beast (Happy Ever After Standalone Novel Series)

Beautiful Girl

Published by Sparklesoup.com

Sparklesoup Inc.

Copyright © 2016 Kailin Gow

Thank you for Purchasing this book!
Get 3 Additional books from Kailin Gow as a Gift!
http://bit.ly/2dXz8Sd

For information, please contact:

Sparklesoup Inc.

11700 W. Charleston Blvd. Ste. 170-95

Las Vegas, NV 89135

www.Sparklesoup.com

First Edition.

Printed in the United States of America

Kailin Gow

Note from Author

Beautiful Girl contains some social issues which symbolize the ugliness of humankind. Hatred rears its ugly "beast" head in this novel in a form that is hurtful and offensive. However, if you will, escape into a world open with possibilities, in *Beautiful Girl*, you might find there might be a cure against hate, and that is love.

Happy Reading Ever After!

Love,

Kailin

Prologue

<u>Mason Beast</u>

My eyes traveled the entire glittering floor of Beast's Department Stores in admiration of how all my hard work had come together tonight, as well as to ensure that every detail was in order. This event was the hallmark of my career and my opportunity to show that I was the future of Beast's Department Stores. And this new store was a flagship store, in our family's own city and community - one that showed just how distinct and high end we were. It was where the headquarters of our billion-dollars conglomerate had moved. Beast's Newport was my "baby" which I built from concept to opening…my first store my father, whose father founded Beast's, put me in charge of. And I was the over protective but proud parent.

Quickly glancing at one of the many mirrors that were present, I was pleased to see that my new black Armani tux was impeccable, along with platinum cufflinks and studs with the small B engraved in them for Beast. My dark hair was in place, my smile bright and white, and my eyes sparkling with just the proper amount of charm to draw in the guests. I was ready.

"Mason, this has come together well," my father said. He'd come up next to me and was looking around with a critical, but satisfied eye. I worked hard to earn those looks and aside from me being satisfied with my efforts, it meant something to have Theodore Beast III satisfied with them, too. And before him, my grandfather had been the exact same way—a dynasty that started in the early 1900s, surviving depressions, recessions, and a few aggressions from angry competitors. The Beast's Department Stores were one of the grand department stores which offered the most refined and high-end luxury brands since the 1900s and served clientele such as the Vanderbilts, European royalties, movie stars, and Asian dignitaries.

"I haven't left any stone unturned," I said.

"I can tell, but you should certainly relax and enjoy yourself now. You've done well," he said.

"I appreciate that, Father," I replied. Before I could say anything else, he turned to talk with a friend and fellow investor in various adventures through their venture capital firm, and I went back to my assessment.

Thirty-two. I was twenty-five years old and this opening was the thirty-second department store that I had attended in my life, from the age of fifteen on, when I really took an interest in business. However, this was the very first one that I'd been in control of—revealing the new look of Beast's to our vendors and the faces of the top lines that we carried.

Breathing in, I grabbed a glass of champagne from the waiter who paused in front of me. "Thank you," I said, nodding at him. He nodded and moved on, eloquently navigating his way through the small pockets of people in deep conversation, laughter echoing in the air.

Kailin Gow

Laughter was good, because people who had fun would remember and then they'd shop. I noticed how the models that were walking around with some of the newest products that would be offered at the Newport store before all others brought an air of eloquence and beauty to the environment. Scents of sweet orange and vanilla wafted through the air from the strategically placed candles. The scents were chosen because of their qualities to bring about good thoughts in a subtle and indirect manner to those who were around them. I couldn't argue that it worked, because I was feeling good.

Over to the right, the "young and hip" crowd lingered, laughing and showing that Beast's was a place for all ages—the elderly wealthy crowd and also the children and grandchildren of that crowd, too. It was a place where people with inherited money were glad to spend it freely and those who were working their way up the ladder of success made it a goal to spend their money at. My goal was to take as much money in as I could from all these people.

Beautiful Girl: Modern Beauty and Beast (Happy Ever After Standalone Novel Series)

It was strange looking at this younger Abercrombie inspired crowd. Many were my age, but in many ways, I felt like an old man next to them. They talked differently than me and had different priorities, too. I couldn't recall ever having a dilemma about what party or club to go to in a given night. For me, it was what line would maximize the potential of something or better use my time so I could take another class or two. Yes, I was considered fairly dull by most, I imagined.

Then I stopped breathing.

On the outskirts of the crowd was a woman who stood out, even among all the "beautiful people" that were at the event. Her eyes flickered with excitement, shooting out sparks of amber and gold. Was it the candles or something that came from within her? I couldn't tell, but I was drawn to her. And her hair, it was long and thick, shimmering like a caramel gold. Her exotic looks were complimented nicely by a friendly smile, making her even more unique.

"Who is she?" Father asked me, leaning in.

"I have no idea, but…"

"Wow," he finished for me. "She stands out like star in a sky."

"Hardly adequate, but still the best choice," I said, my voice low and my eyes not losing sight of the exquisite prize they'd landed upon.

"You should go greet our guest, Mason."

"There's too much to attend to." My words were weak and my argument pretty lame.

"Well, you can't stop staring at her and she is at your party. You should find out who she is. And maybe— just maybe—you will be the son who provides me a grandchild before I die. God knows Callum is too busy chasing every skirt around to ever settle down—at least not for a long time."

Beautiful Girl: Modern Beauty and Beast (Happy Ever After Standalone Novel Series)

"And I'm too busy with work to entertain getting serious about a girl. She's beautiful, but if she doesn't have brains, I'm not interested. And from the looks of it, very few people here are known for their brains."

"Really?" my father said, leaning in. "I know you're the more steady one of my two boys, but I also know, you have been on dates before. Remember, I was a young man long ago, too. I know what young men like you and Callum are all about when it comes to ladies. Go talk to this girl. You haven't even looked at me while I've been talking to you. See what it's all about, Mason."

I thought about what Dad said. It was correct, of course, and if I didn't make my way over there, Callum probably would. Well, at least it would answer my curiosity about brains—Callum didn't like brainy women at all. As for me, I liked smart women, especially if they were smarter than me. She would be an asset, if she was. Unfortunately or fortunately it was a small number of women that were, to the best of my knowledge.

Callum's loud laugh erupted from the room, taking my eyes away from the mysterious woman. There was Callum, charming his groupies who were eager to be associated with him, hoping that they'd maybe end up in a photograph near him—their brush with fame. Where I looked for the Warren Buffet's of the world, these people looked for underwear models, which was basically Callum's role in our family's business building empire.

"By the way," Father added. It was only when he spoke that I realized he was still there. "How's the latest ad campaign going?"

"Good, I suppose. He's wearing nothing and covered up with a strategically placed flag," I snickered.

"Please tell me he's not exposing himself," Father mumbled.

"No," I said. I didn't bother mentioning the Facebook picture where the flag was a bit too low, showing a bit too much, and certain parts of his body on the verge of saluting. Women had loved it, which definitely made Callum become more of an exhibitionist with each passing week, it seemed. He loved the attention. And as for me, I loved the money that the attention my big brother got brought into the store.

It's time to go meet this guest, I thought. I handed over an empty champagne glass to a waiter and grabbed two new glasses and made my way over there. My ears were alert, trying to tune in and hear her voice, but I couldn't. Then, almost in slow motion despite my purpose and quick stride, I was there.

The young woman was standing there, looking sophisticated and understated in a simple black dress that was tight and hugged her obviously well worked out curves. She was talking with an attractive Asian woman, in a long silk red gown and lots of jewelry on. She looked to be in her late 40s in my opinion—and without any work done. I felt anticipation about the introduction and it was hard to ignore. "Hi, excuse me," I said. "I don't believe that I've had the pleasure of meeting either of you before. I'm Mason Beast, the organizer of this event. I hope you're enjoying this party. Champagne?" I offered the two glasses and each woman took one, both glancing at each other and wearing a very similar smile on their faces.

"It's a pleasure to meet the man behind this beautiful store," the older woman began. "I'm Helen Chu of Chu Cosmetics. And this is my daughter Charisma."

"Thank you," I said, "for both the compliment and in the introduction. I fear none should have been needed, as you are quite well known and respected."

"You're too kind," Helen said, but my eyes were on Charisma, again. It felt like part of my soul would be yanked out of my chest if I turned away. Those amber eyes—so alluring. Yes, she was distinct and beautiful—a different type of beauty than others that were given that term. Hers was real and authentic, outward and inward, too.

"I bet this took a while to plan," Charisma said. "What inspire the look of this store versus others?"

"Well, the flagship stores need to be…"

I was cut off by an unwelcomed, deep voice behind me. "The ocean, sweetheart. That's where the inspiration comes from..." I turned around and saw Callum there, which instantly irritated me. His arrogance had no place in my conversation. Then he leaned in and touched Charisma, which irritated me, but I quickly grew more amused by her reaction. She flinched and pulled back. Apparently someone was immune to the charms of Callum Beast. It added even more to her appeal.

Callum had a quick flicker of disappointment on his face, but it was replaced with a snide arrogance in a nanosecond. "Oh, don't worry sweetheart, I won't touch you. I don't need you. I've got plenty of girls who would faint from just my touch. Pretty girls, classy girls, and certainly girls much younger than this woman here," he said, pulling Helen toward him and scanning her in a highly inappropriate way. "And they sure as hell have bigger, rounder eyes than yours," he said.

"Callum," I said in a low, irritated voice. What the hell was he doing?

He ignored me and snapped his fingers instead. Like loyal dogs, two girls came over to him and draped their arms around him like he was some sort of god. He looked at the two and then to Helen and Charisma and said, "Girls, never dress yourself like some cheap kung fu fighting nail technician like this woman here. Who let this second rate wannabe in the store?"

"Callum, that's enough," I cautioned. I wished he'd just leave. Not only was he was being such a prick, he was showing a really ugly side to him that was embarrassing and unforgivable. I didn't know I had such a hateful brother. His model black hair and infamous green eyes didn't impress me, and neither did his decorum. He was being ugly.

I put my hand on his arm and tried to pull him away, but I was met with resistance. Helen Chu was grabbing his other arm and pulling him toward her. And her eyes may be small according to Callum, but they were shooting out intense sparks that looked like she was ready to light him up. It made me curious, I'll admit, but I hoped that no one would cause a scene. The soiree didn't need that.

"Son, you better be drunk so you have a good excuse on why you said all those nasty things to me. Otherwise, you're a hateful person and I pity you."

Callum laughed, trying to blow it off, but his arm candy was completely paying attention to Helen Chu, and likely wearing her make-up line, too.

"You think you know it all just because you're the son of a billionaire? You think you know what people are like? How to run a business? How to judge character? Guess again. First of all, you don't know what beauty is if you call those sleazy girls flanking your side beautiful."

Now the girls went from smug curiosity to feigned insult.

"Second, you just insulted a whole lot of people when you called my eyes small and assume all people like me are kung fu fighting nail technicians. Besides, you got the wrong nationality. I'm Chinese, and many of us do not work at a nail salon. Kung fu originated by the Chinese, and not all Asians know it. And you wouldn't know what is cheap or classy any day since you have never had any real life experience picking out your own clothes or knowing how hard those nail technicians worked. And underwear is hardly classy. So…despite being a Beast, you're insignificant, certainly more than any nail technician out there, or even a bum on the street. Your superiority complex may be accepted in some circles, but not in this one," Helen said, making a circle with her hand.

I felt heat rise up my neck and I knew that the tension in this small circle was quite obvious. Callum's behavior was inexcusable, too, and potentially costly.

"Whatever. You look like you should be serving cocktails at a cabaret show, not *here*," Callum said. He waved his hand dismissively and quickly found out what a bad mistake that was.

"You can swat your hand like a princess, but let me tell you, you don't know who I am and your lack of class may just cost your family big."

Again, Callum snorted. I felt I should step in, but truthfully, my big brother needed this type of interaction with a woman who didn't look at him as the end-all of masculine perfection.

"I'm Helen Chu and the owner of the company that makes your newest cosmetics brand. Your father just made a deal with me to carry a full line of my products in every store. We've partnered up, but I may need to reconsider that. I don't do business with people who have no ethics or moral compass—which clearly seems to be you."

Now I wanted to panic. "Callum, you owe Helen an apology. This is uncalled for," I said.

"Never," he said, glaring at me.

"An apology is hardly a judge of heart. So, Mr. Hotshot, here's an ugly little truth for you to dwell on. I'm the big investor on that little film you want to make— the one where I am the Executive Producer, so you'll be seeing a lot more of me and…"

Callum cut her off, his voice escalating an octave. "Oh hell no. You will not be an Executive Producer. I don't associate with new money for what…being a nail technician?"

"You signed the deal and unlike you, I'm the one heading this film. You can be replaced more quickly than I can," Helen said.

"I'll pay you your money back," Callum said, shrugging his shoulders. I could tell that he wasn't sure how to take this. Business was not his forte, it was mine. And I had no problems believing that Helen Chu was masterful at business, understanding the value of her time, money, and efforts.

Beautiful Girl: Modern Beauty and Beast (Happy Ever After Standalone Novel Series)

"I don't buy it. You wouldn't have had to have a Kickstarter campaign for your movie if it had any real merit from the get-go. The first Kickstarter, you failed to bring in even a $1000 for your $20 million film. Then you tried again with an IndieGoGo campaign and failed halfway through. Your father came to me to see if I wanted to invest as one of the investors. Being generous and having good relations with my business partners, I said I'll fund the entire thing. Even you—billionaire playboy—couldn't get your family to back it. There's a reason for that and I certainly know that it isn't because you wanted to do things the hard way and earn it."

"You don't know shit," Callum said.

Helen just smiled and then breathed in, before calmly saying, "Until you see and appreciate what you have, and find out what true beauty and self-worth is, you deserve a rude awakening to knock some sense into you." Then she took Charisma's hand and walked away.

I wanted to run after them, but the moment was so heated that there were no words that I could say that would offset what Callum had done. I'd have to put some effort, thought, and time into coming up with a solution. It was possible that he lost us our strongest new partner with his rude manners and arrogant demeanor. And if he did, well, he'd have a lot more to deal with than he had just ten minutes ago.

Dad showed up the next second, probably witness to the debacle. "What the hell happened here?"

I looked at Callum and he was looking at Dad, his two bimbos giggling next to him. Dad looked irritated and I didn't blame him. I'd let him scold Callum for this one, because that would be the only way Callum would listen—even a little bit.

"You better not have upset Helen Chu," he cautioned. "You know how long we've been trying to get her to come to our stores so we can carry her line. She's the fastest growing cosmetics and fashion business globally."

"She'll cheapen our stores, Father," Callum said.

"Why would you say that?" he asked, glaring at him. "Are you questioning my business judgment?"

For most people, this would have been dangerous territory, but not for my brother, the clueless dolt.

"She's self-made, not someone of distinction," Callum said.

"You damn fool," Father said. "You had better not have done any irreparable harm. Self-made is even more impressive because it shows more hard work, ingenuity, and perseverance than someone who just inherited wealth, like you. Everyone who became 'someone of distinction' was self-made at one point." Then Father turned to me—his clean-up man. "Did you have anything to do with this? Did you insult Helen, too?"

"No," I said, shocked that he'd even think that. "I had nothing to do with anything this damn fool did. I'm not responsible for the stupidity that comes out of his mouth, Dad. I'm ashamed to be called his brother for calling Mrs. Chu what he did. If he is the face of Beast's, then he just about showed everyone the ugliest face we can be – racist. This stupid fool just alienated more than half of the human population, and he also had no respect for women and hard-working people. As far as this gala, everything is shot. She was a distinguished guest this evening and it's clear that something went on. We have the press here. We have her fans, which I reached out to invite. If they hear one thing from Helen Chu, who is more well-known than we are, as a brand name cosmetics and fashion line around the world, our business would tank. Now…"

Father grabbed Callum and pulled him close. "You fix this or you are no longer my son."

Chapter 1

<u>Charisma</u>

I'd never been so shocked and offended by anything in my life, and that was saying quite a bit considering some of the jackasses I'd met over the years at school and in the various neighborhoods Mom and I had lived in.

"I can't believe that brute!" I hissed. "Where does he get off thinking he can talk that way to you—to anyone, really? Who does he think he is?"

"He thinks that just because he's Callum Beast, he can do whatever he wants. Well, his name means nothing to me and just being handed wealth is not impressive. He clearly lacks integrity, which should embarrass his father. Perhaps I misjudged Theodore Beast III. I thought he had integrity, but his son certainly doesn't show it."

"And he's an underwear model," I said.

"True, Charisma. But the company he models for puts up with a lot, because in exchange they get good store location for their product. He's too full of himself to realize he's being used," Mom said.

"I'm sorry this happened to you, Mom. It makes me so angry. I swear that if I ever see him again I might just slap him and call him a jerk, because that's what he is."

"You don't need to be overprotective of me. I've dealt with plenty of people like him in my life. They always get what's coming to them—in one way or another," Mom said.

"Well, he deserves whatever he gets. His brother seemed okay, not that we got to talk much. But what he did ruined their entire event and caused quite the scene. The media will have a field day with it. Surprised they're not calling you already," I said.

"Lucy will tend to it if they do," Mom said. Lucy was her personal secretary. "But I'd better fill her in so she knows what's happening."

While Mom was on her phone with Lucy, composed and purpose driven with her instructions, I was still fuming. I just couldn't believe that anyone would have such inexcusable behavior. Didn't the guy have a filter? He may have been considered one of the most physically beautiful men in the world, but inside, he was an ugly individual—shallow and incapable of human decency.

***

Well, my night had been cut short so I thought it would be a good time to catch up on the beauty blog and my youtube channel showcasing how to use the products, which was my responsibility for Mom's business. I love doing it so I could showcase Mom's products and also her achievements. I was so proud of her and I always remembered, even as a kid, how special it was that she worked so hard for a better life for her—for us.

After replying to a few comments on the blog, I went to a report that I receive daily to show when either Helen Chu or Chu Cosmetics was mentioned online. We had a spike in comments and mentions. All about the Beast's Newport Opening event and Callum Beast. Oh boy, the incident had only been an hour ago and it had already caught fire in the virtual world.

I began to investigate and my stomach sank. "Oh no! What is this guy's problem?" Callum Beast was in all-out jerk mode. Not only was there a blow up of news about him, but he was fueling the fire. As though he was proud of being a racist jerk.

> *Shared my mind with low-class bitch who calls herself the cosmetics queen and she walked out of her own party.* #HelenChuCosmeticsCheap

> *Cheap Helen Chu has cheap knock-off cosmetics. Wouldn't buy anything made in Chu.* #HelenChuCosmeticsCheap

Beautiful Girl: Modern Beauty and Beast (Happy Ever After Standalone Novel Series)

Driving my father home from a botched gala. Peeps—not my fault it fell. Blame the crazy bitch. #HelenChuCosmeticsCheap

Don't care if #HelenChuCosmeticsCheap *is funding the full budget for a top secret film I'm doing, she will not be my Executive Producer.*

I was mad and offended by what I'd seen. My mother did absolutely nothing to him to have him pick on her and call her vile things. The only reason he was picking on her was because of what she was born as. He should be picking on me, too, except I looked more like my father, who was anglo, than Mom.

Mom better not see this or who knows what she'll do, I thought. I wanted to go off on a rant like the appropriately named Beast did, but I was better than that and Mom would definitely not be happy with me if I did it. "Decorum is important, Charisma." I don't know how many times I'd heard her say that. So, knowing it was best to lie low, I took solace in Mom's words of caution to heart. She was always eager to throw ancient wisdom and folklore in with modern life situations. And when Callum

Beast got his comeuppance, I'd be there smiling about it. Jerk!

Okay, maybe one thing, I thought.

@TheCallum, you have widened my small exotic eyes tonight. Hope you get everything you deserve.

What a jerk, thinking all Asians have small eyes. Mine was practically manga size, meaning too large for my face. And so were many of the girls who modeled for us in our Asian division. It goes to show how wrong and off base stereotypes were. After my feed, it was silent. It seemed too good to be true that it had done the trick and shut up the arrogant ass, but fortune was on my side. Maybe he'd broken a nail and had to get an emergency manicure or something—from a kung fu fighting nail tech.

After a shower to further calm me down, I ran back out into my bedroom to my phone ringing away. I didn't recognize the number, though.

"Hello," I said, a bit winded.

"Charisma?" someone said, in more of a question, really.

"Yes, this is she."

"Hi, this is Mason Beast. Do you have a minute?"

I glanced at the clock. It was late, but I had a minute. Should be interesting to hear what he had to say. "Sure."

"I apologize for the late hour, Charisma, but on behalf of the Beast Company and my father, I apologize for Callum's horrendous behavior tonight. He can be a jerk, granted, but tonight he was in rare form—even by his standards. We're not sure why, but we're trying to get to the bottom of it."

"He's part of your image, your brand," I said, not wanting to let Mason off easy. It wasn't his fault, but what I said was true. Callum was the "look" of Beast Brands.

"Agreed, but what he said is not reflected by anyone else, and I hope to God not him, either. And the way he acted wasn't acceptable. If he wasn't family, he'd be fired. Can you come in tomorrow with your mother Helen so we can discuss a way The Beast Company can make it up to you?"

He clearly wasn't his brother and we owed him that. After all, he'd put a lot of work into the event. "It's clear you are not the same as your brother, Mason. I'll tell my mom about the meeting tomorrow. What your brother did was truly offensive, though, and I think it would be in everyone's best interests if he was not present at the meeting."

"Agreed," Mason said. I was pretty sure he sounded relieved about that and in agreement. Maybe I shouldn't have let them off so easy and insisted Callum be there and have to keep his big, fat mouth shut.

"Okay then," I said.

There was a small silence and finally Mason spoke again. "I really do want you to know that I don't feel the same way and I'm ashamed to call Callum my brother. We're nothing alike and I've always known that, but it has never been as apparent as it was tonight."

"I can tell," I said.

He continued talking despite me accepting his words at face value. I guess he just had to get it all off his chest, maybe. "Sadly, my brother is ignorant of your mother's success and everything in general. He insulted a very nice and good lady, and I just can't stand for that. If I ever take control of this company, I will make sure he gets put in his place. I feel quite confident that he'll get what's due to him. People who act that way always do."

I felt bad for Mason. It must be tough having an older brother like Callum. Made me glad to be an only child. "Well, I'm sorry to hear how tough it is on you, Mason."

"My father is talking to him right now, while Callum drives him home. Father seemed serious about having Callum fixed what he's done about your mom, and if he doesn't, he would disown him. That's how sorry we are about all this. And how serious we are to keep your products in all of our stores. Good night, Charisma."

Whether it was just a PR call or a genuine apology, I admired how Mason had handled it. He seemed quite sincere and I felt drawn to the way he said my name. There was a soft sigh in the way he said it and it was strangely intriguing. Men had always paid attention to me, but I could tell which ones were true gentlemen, and I sensed a gentleman in Mason. Plus, he was very handsome and wore a tux which made him look so suave like James Bond.

I'd planned on working on my graduate paper that evening, but found myself distracted by Mason's call. I'd just have to work on it tomorrow after the meeting. The paper was ahead of schedule for my professors at USC, but graduation from the MBA program would be happening soon enough so I could not slack off.

Chapter 2

Callum Beast

As I blinked my eyes and tried to focus, I couldn't understand why Father and Mason were so mad about what happened with Helen Chu and that gorgeous babe next to her. If they couldn't take a joke—screw them. I thought it was damn funny, and everyone else should have, too. That was the problem with uptights; they lacked a sense of humor and didn't enjoy all the great things that had to laugh about when money wasn't a concern.

I walked into the back room of the store, the soon to be executive suite, and saw my buds, Terry Snod and Sherman Temple sitting there, each snorting lines of coke. After college, they'd gone the Wall Street route, but they liked to party just like they did during the frat days— screwing beautiful women and enjoying some of the best drugs. Earlier, they'd given me some ecstasy and a little pot. Must have been some good stuff, because I was still fuzzy from it. Add in the champagne, and I was definitely flying high.

"Man, you were supposed to come back with some women for us. Hot, horny, and desperate women who are endowed with tits and money from their parents," Terry said. Then he went right back down to the mirror in front of him.

"Shit, had a SNAFU," I said.

"Yeah, what? Nothing messed up ever happens to you, underwear man," Sherman said, leaning back and looking at me.

"Some Asian bitch, Helen Chu, didn't have a sense of humor is all. My dad and brother busted my ass for it."

"The cosmetics woman?" Terry said. "Man, her stock has soared ever since she went IPO. Would love to have her for a client."

"Maybe she wouldn't be so uptight if you slipped her the big one," I said. Then I smirked. "Or little one; little like her eyes."

Again, only I laughed. What the hell was wrong with people?

"Um, you have to check your eyes, Man," Terry said. "Helen Chu is your Dad's age, but look barely 30, and her eyes are so gorgeous they had a feature on them in Vogue."

"She wouldn't have sold the most eye makeup this year in Cosmetics if she didn't have gorgeous eyes," Sherman said. "You sound like a jerk, you know, Callum."

My friends' disapproval of me only mad me angrier so I pulled out my phone and decided to spread a little Chu dislike on my Twitter. I'd enjoy every delightful second of my faithful following siding with me and bashing her. But I also lost a ton of followers right after my Tweet.

No sooner did I get a few Tweets out then the door opened up. My eyes widened, not wanting anyone to see the drugs. It was Dad and he barely stuck his head around the corner. He demanded, "Callum. Hallway. Now."

"When the master calls, I listen," I said, more to Terry and Sherman, but Dad heard it, too, and frowned even further. He looked damn tense, like he might have a heart attack or something.

"Yeah," I said. I was aware that my voice was slightly slurred and hoped that he couldn't tell.

"Son, you embarrassed the whole company and family with your racist and dumb remarks earlier. It is inexcusable."

"But…" I began, but Father raised his hand and shut me down.

"Your mother and I have taught you better than that. You're going to have to make up for what you did. We're leaving right now and hoping we can catch Ms. Chu and her daughter before they get home and make this right. Do you understand?"

"No, I don't. Why is it my problem that they couldn't take a joke," I said, crossing my arms. His voice faded in and out like I was lifting my head in and out of water.

"That was no joke, Callum," he said, smacking me on the head, which made my head spin even more. "If you would have said that to anyone else, they would have beaten you to a pulp. You said it to an innocent woman who had a rough life until she worked hard to pull herself up to the success she is today. She's the kind of person we, as men of good fortune, are supposed to protect and support. The more we have, the more we are supposed to be benevolent and kind. Haven't you learned that lesson at all? If not, I failed as a parent. Today, you've really disappointed me, Callum."

"Ok, okay," I said, shaking my spinning head. "What do you want me to do?"

"What the hell is the matter with you?" Father said, trying to control his voice. "I just told you. We're going to go after them right now and try to straighten out this mess."

"Now? It can wait," I said.

"No, it can't. This will be taken care of tonight." Then Father grabbed my arm and showed me that I would be leaving with him at that moment. Conversation over.

On the way out, we went past Mason, and Father filled him in. The way Mason looked at me was irritating. He was my younger brother and his condescending look was out of place. He'd best be served to remember who the head of the Beast enterprises would be some day. Me—number one, and him, number two, if I was nice enough to let him stay there.

***

Standing in front of the Bentley Continental in the underground parking garage, Dad tossed me the keys and commanded, "Drive."

I shouldn't have been driving, but I wasn't about to argue. His swift action had resonated even in my fuzzy head. He was damn serious and this was not the time to push it. So off I went, down the highway at a break neck speed trying to catch up with the nobody who'd ruined my evening. It was so bogus!

At first I thought that Dad would quiet down when we got into the car, but I was wrong. He talked and talked, only pausing to breathe. "You are the eldest son and should have been setting an example tonight, representing the family in a professional way. But you didn't. You have a responsibility as the golden boy—the face of Beast Company—and need to watch your public image more. The publicity from this is going to be atrocious."

"I thought all publicity was good publicity, Father."

"No, it's not, not when it's an embarrassment to the family and to our organization. I'd like to retire some day, but can't do that until I know that you and Mason can handle the company on your own. You've got to grow up and stop being so vain, and thinking with your dick."

I sighed, not sure what to say. I knew that he had a point and really, the last thing I wanted to do was have my father disapprove of me. Tonight had been a disaster and it probably was the drugs talking, but I couldn't tell him that. Quite the conundrum.

"Callum, are you listening?"

"Yes."

"Good. You are not a college playboy anymore. You're a grown man with real life responsibilities. You're about to become an heir to one of the biggest enterprises in America—in charge of carrying on the legacy of the Beast name."

I'd heard all of this before, of course. I'd hoped to have as much fun as I could before having to get serious with all of that, but Father clearly had a different idea. "What if I don't meet your expectations?" I asked.

Father sighed and reached over to pat my shoulder. "I have every faith that you will, but it's just a matter of how long and how much it will take to get your there, son. I love you and Mason very much, but when it comes down to it, I have to make the choice of who runs the company based on who is best at it. As of this moment, Mason is doing a better job at it than you are."

"How could that be? I do everything—model, appear at events, meet people, and am constantly bringing exposure to Beast Stores. Mason is a paper pusher. He looks at figures…"

"What he does behind the scenes is equally important," Father immediately countered. "It is my wish that you and he will begin working together and both of you will use your talents and skills to peacefully and successfully run this business. Two brothers can run the Beast Company, but it seems our alpha males always get competitive when challenged. And from the looks of it, both you and Mason were challenged tonight. About the store, and about…that girl."

"That girl?" I asked, feeling my lip curling up in a sneer. "You can't be serious. She's not even my type…the girl next to Ms. Chu."

"She's got something regal about her," my father said. "She's Ms. Chu's daughter, you know, and she's getting her MBA from USC like Mason did, and she's helped her mom get Helen Chu Cosmetics distributed worldwide—all at a young age. That girl has looks, brains, and gumption—something that is sorely lacking in many young adults today. If she wasn't already Helen Chu's daughter, I would adopt her and bring her onboard. Kids these days feel so entitled. But not her. She was brought up right, and…"

"Obviously you think highly of her, Dad," I said. It took a lot to impress Theodore Beast III and this girl had managed to do it without so much as having a conversation with him. "So, you playing matchmaker for Mason?"

"Why Mason? I'm talking about you, Callum. A girl like that will make a man of you yet."

"Dad," I protested. "She's not my type and I don't need a matchmaker."

"Any girl who is not a floozy is not your type. You are in your late twenties, Callum. It's time you grow up. I'm tired of holding your hand. Will I always be there for you? Of course, but as a parent it is my wish to see you grow into a mature, responsible, and kind person—not someone who bullies older ladies and puts down people who are less fortunate. You have really disappointed me tonight, son, with the hurtful words you said to Ms. Chu. You didn't even know what you were talking about. She's had a harsh life and it took a lot to build herself up to where she is now. She should be respected and admired, not treated so poorly."

"I know, I know, it embarrassed you," I said.

"Worse than that, it shamed me, Callum. It's going to take more than an apology to set this one right. It's going to take action and proving that you don't have a dark heart."

"I told you, it was just a joke."

"And I call bullshit. It wasn't."

Now I felt bad and the more my head cleared up, the worse it became. My eyes started to tear up. I didn't like that I'd hurt and embarrassed my father. I wanted him to be proud of me. Before a tear could escape down my cheek, I reached up and wiped my eye.

I didn't see the curve ahead until it was too late. The car hit something and stopped instantly with a force that propelled me forward. I felt my body hurling through

the windshield and sharp pain everywhere. Then darkness
set in.

Chapter 3

<u>Mason</u>

Standing in the hospital waiting room, I pulled my bowtie off from my shirt and stuffed it into my tuxedo pocket. Mother was standing off to the right, just staring at nothing and playing with her strand of pearls. I walked over to her and tried to comfort her, but no words could really be spoken that were adequate. Callum had crashed the car and now he and Father were in critical condition.

"I just don't understand," my mother mumbled.

"Sometimes there are no explanations for this, Mom," I offered.

She looked at me with such pain in her large blue eyes. "Mason, I just never thought I'd be standing here, waiting for someone to tell me I could see your father. We've always been so fortunate."

"And we will be again," I offered. Sadly, I didn't really believe that, because I saw how the staff was glancing at us and running in and out of the room where Callum was. Father was in surgery for internal bleeding. "Let's go get some coffee. Maybe we can visit them when we get back up here, okay."

She nodded and I went and told the attending nurse. When we came back, a nurse was pointing in our direction, talking to a doctor. "See, they're ready for us," I said.

The doctor walked up to us and a somber look was on his face. He was tall, but he seemed to stare at the floor when he spoke. "I'm sorry. We tried, but your husband didn't make it through surgery."

Instinctually, my arms wrapped around my mother's as I felt her body go limp and begin shaking. I guided her to a chair and the doctor kept talking, but what did the words matter. *He didn't make it.* That was all I kept hearing.

"Can I see him?" Mother asked.

"Yes, of course."

I got up to guide her and we walked down the corridor and toward a room in the distance. My eyes stung and my heart was racing, as I thought about how much my family had changed that evening. And all because of Callum being a pompous ass.

We walked into the room and there he was—Theodore Beast III, the man who'd always been mightier than life to me—lying there with a gray complexion and cuts all over his face and body from the windshield's glass. Mother started to weep, overwhelmed.

I couldn't help but cry, too. It was so damn unfair and I felt such excruciating pain swelling up in my chest, but in my mind, I was so angry.

"How is Callum doing?" I heard my mother ask. I didn't care at that moment. Because of him, our family had been permanently changed.

"He's still out of it and pretty banged up. He's young enough that he should rebound, but he'll have an uphill climb. His face is broken in four spots and has a lot of abrasions on it. There's a lot of stitches."

"Can I see him?" Mother asked, grabbing my hand for support.

"Yes, but I want to warn you, it may be tough to look at him. He's swollen and bandaged and...not the same as what you are used to seeing," the doctor said.

"But he'll survive?" Mother asked hesitantly.

"It's touch and go right now. With the way the leg and hip broke, a permanent limp is highly possible and as far as his face, I'm not certain how much reconstructive surgeries will help due to the severity," the doctor offered softly.

"Just so long as he survives," she whispered.

I listened to this and felt myself growing angrier with every word. Callum had caused everyone so much pain. It was horrible, but I was glad that he'd had such a bad accident and it would cause him problems. He needed to be knocked off his high horse.

The doctor guided us over to Callum's room, saying that we could go in, but I took a pass, not wanting to see my brother and fearful that my hatred would show on my face and mother would take note of it. I didn't want that to happen.

Standing in the hallway, my back pressed against the sterile white wall, I tried to process it all—so many emotions and one lingering thought. The business…what would happen to Beast Companies? I knew for sure that I'd do everything in my power to not have Callum take over as CEO. He'd ruin generations' worth of work and from the sound of it, underwear model was no longer in his future. *No, he will not ruin this family's legacy*, I thought.

***

Four weeks later...

Life had been a whirlwind of activities. Burying Father. Dealing with the press from Callum's activities. He'd become the male Lindsey Lohan to many— everyone curious about his bad behavior and drawn to every gritty detail of it. But the headlines in the gossip magazines blaming him for my father's death were the worst. They were harsh and I thought they were true.

I'd been named temporary CEO of the company, not able to persuade the board to use common sense over following the instructions that Father had in place. So...I was there, but would have to work hard to make sure that Callum never became the face behind the position. It was too risky. The first decision I had was to delay the opening of the flagship store for a month. It was challenging and met with opposition, but I felt like it would be an unwelcomed media circus and that wasn't going to be acceptable. Some other well known face would do something ridiculous and take the pressure of Callum before then, and that would be good for us.

Finally, Callum was released from the hospital. We had him set up with home health care and the ugliest nurse I could find, just to make sure he didn't do anything stupid too soon. To the best of my abilities, I was leaving no stone unturned, and that included the beautiful Charisma Chu.

Chapter 4

Charisma

The news about what had happened to the Beast family on the very night they'd insulted my mother and me was shocking for me. However, for the media, it was a sensational story, one that had every element they loved—tragedy, drama, shock, and intense emotions. On Facebook, Instagram, and Twitter, the messages that Callum had said about Helen Chu Cosmetics were trending in all the newsfeeds. It was easily managed with a bit of PR, and also helped by the fact that Callum Beast was under investigation for being under the influence when he was driving that evening. Apparently a combination of alcohol and some other drugs. He'd paid a heavy price for it—losing his father and becoming quite deformed physically, from what I understood. One headline had been particularly cruel: The Beauty is Definitely a Beast Now.

Beautiful Girl: Modern Beauty and Beast (Happy Ever After Standalone Novel Series)

Today I was finally meeting with Mason, two weeks after the accident. I knew why the meeting was important to him, but he had no idea why it was important to me. I had an agenda, too.

***

"Mason, hi," I said, smiling at him as he stood up from the table at Rendezvous, a trendy French restaurant.

"Charisma, thanks for your patience," he said. I stared at him and saw an appreciative look in his eyes. I'd seen it before, but I also saw that there was a gentleman in there that was able to control the beast within, if you will—pun intended. "Please, have a seat."

He held out the seat for me and then sat back down. I looked at him and was curious if I'd see stress and sorrow from all that had happened the last few weeks, but I saw a man who was very composed. I was impressed and mildly curious about it for some reason. Not sure why…it wasn't like I wanted him to break down weeping and have me come to the rescue and reassure him he'd be fine and then make hot, passionate love to him. Whoa! Where did that come from?

"I hope you're doing well," I said.

"Fair enough. Been some pretty long days, but everything's coming together...feeling a bit more normal."

"That's good to hear," I said. "When is Callum expected to be able to go home?"

"In a week or two," Mason said. Then he changed the subject. "Well, originally this meeting was to apologize to your mother and you, but that's been adjusted a bit. I just want you to know, that regardless of all that's unfolded, I am personally truly sorry about it."

"All is forgiven. It's 'water under the bridge,' as they say. Actually, I have something to discuss with you, Mason."

"You do?" he asked, raising an eyebrow.

"Yes, it involves my final work for my MBA."

"Soon to be a fellow USC alum. That's great. Tough program, but rewarding."

"Agreed," I said. It was nice to meet a guy who loved a woman with brains, or at least wasn't intimidated by them. Mason Beast was known to be one of the most astute graduates of the program, but I hoped to best him, if at all possible.

"So, what is it that I can do for you, Charisma?"

"I am hoping that Beast Company will help me with my thesis. The topic is Managing Change in a Corporation."

"And you didn't want to do your mother's company?"

"Initially, yes, but my advisor said no. After I reflected upon it, it makes sense. So, I am hoping that I can spend a little time at Beast Company and use it as the subject of the thesis. What do you think?"

Mason looked at me and I could practically hear the wheels turning in his mind. He finally said, in a rather soft and personal voice, compared to that "business meeting tone, "We've certainly been going through changes." Then he paused and I didn't speak, realizing it may be too bold of a request at the moment. Then his lips slowly opened and I watched them like they were moving in slow motion. "Yes, but on one condition."

Oh no, conditions, I thought. "Which is what, Mason?"

"Helen Chu Cosmetics still agrees to do business with us."

"Well, I don't have the final say in that, but I will certainly ask. We haven't really discussed it the past few weeks. There's been *a lot* going on."

"I'm guessing some serious PR thanks to Callum.
I can relate," Mason said. I sensed the hostility in his
voice. There was definitely some bad blood going on
between him and his brother. Had it been there previous
to the past few weeks?

"I don't mean to pry, but..." I began, "I heard he
had some drug problems. Is he getting help for that? It
explains a lot."

"He's dried out by hospitalization, but on so many
pain meds there that I don't really know. He's not by the
store, that's what's important to me. I am not interested
in any more of those embarrassing situations. I'm sure
you can relate."

I nodded my head. I sensed that Callum was a
topic that was preferably off limits with Mason and I was
going to respect that. It wasn't so bad to focus on him as
a man. He was handsome, smart, and successful, and he
had a great body. Really, he was the type of guy that I
always pictured myself ending up with.

We'd already taken care of business before lunch even arrived at the table, which meant that for the rest of the lunch, we talked on a more personal level and about USC, of course. Mason was an interesting guy. He was a fairly decent pianist, played Polo, and was passionate about travel. But he did it smartly, incorporating it in with business. The guy was speaking my language, so I was all too disappointed when the meal had ended, because I felt this chemistry between us that excited me. It was new and different for me, which was good.

"You can have your mother call me directly," Mason said.

"I will. I'll try to connect with her right after this," I said.

Then he extended his hand out and I took it, feeling its warmth masculinity as he shook it, but he didn't release it. He just looked at me for a second, but it felt like an eternity, yet it wasn't awkward.

"Excellent, and email me your agenda of when you'd like to come over to Beast Company and I'll let all the relevant people know. You'll have access to whatever you need," Mason said.

Including you, I thought. Yes, that was a benefit of this paper. I'd get to spend time with this guy. I liked the idea a lot!

"I really enjoyed this lunch, Charisma."

"It was nice. Really, it was just what I needed. I'm glad we could finally connect."

"So, you liked Rendezvous?" he asked.

I nodded.

"Well, you might really like this other place that's near the new store. It has this amazing seven-layer chocolate cake. If you like chocolate, you'll fall in love with it."

"Is that an invitation for cake?" I asked, smiling at him.

"It is."

"That's good, Mason, because it just so happens that I love chocolate cake. It's a weakness, for certain."

"Something else we have in common," he said.

Then he lifted my hand up to his lips and softly kissed it sending a wave of pleasure through me and conjuring an instant vision of those lips on every part of my body.

"Well Charisma, until later," he said.

"Bye," I said and then he held my car door open and I slid into the driver's seat. He closed the door and waved and smiled, standing in the same spot until I drove off.

***

Later that night I approached Mom about my paper. "Okay, Mom, here's the deal. Beast Company will let me do my thesis on them, but only if you still keep the cosmetics agreement with them."

"That Mason is a smart man," she replied, shaking her head. "He obviously understands my commitment to my daughter just as much as he does my commitment to business."

"What do you mean?" I asked.

"I mean that I'll keep my cosmetics line there, because I want you to have your best chance with your thesis. Beast Company is a good company for that project, especially considering all that's happened."

"I guess Callum is in pretty rough shape," I said.

"It's too bad when things like that happen, especially when they are unavoidable," Mom said. She had a matter-of-fact tone. When senseless things happened, she usually had something like that to say.

"You just never know, do you?"

"Every moment is a gift not to be squandered. Speaking of, how were your moments at lunch with that handsome Mason?"

"Really good, actually. He is so different from his brother—a complete gentleman. Plus, he's really interesting. We have a lot in common."

"Good looking, too," Mom said as she gave me a knowing smile. "It sounds like he treated you very well, yes?"

"Yes," I said, laughing. "We're going out for chocolate cake sometime."

"When?"

"Mom, I don't know when."

"If Mason treats you like a princess, then accept it for what it is. He is being a charming businessman like his father and grandfather before him. Just make sure not to fall for him emotionally."

"Mother knows best," I said with a smirk.

"Indeed," she said quite seriously.

After Mom left, I went to my laptop and sent Mason a message answering his question about keeping Helen Chu Cosmetics at Beast's. All my thoughts led to Mason, though, and as a result, Callum, too. Mason was quite a charmer. He was polite, earnest, and such a gentleman. On the other hand, Callum, was such a dirtbag. They were brought up the same way, yet you could not tell they were brothers. They were so different from each other.

Chapter 5

Charisma

I shouldn't have been so nervous about it, but I was. What should I wear? I wanted to look professional, of course, but I was also very aware that a part of me wanted to look good for Mason, too. I liked the way he looked at me and through his green eyes I saw that he respected me, as well as thought I was attractive. I didn't have a lot of experience with dating, because there were so few good options out there, but I knew enough to know that Mason wanted more from me besides a working relationship. A boss and employee relationship wasn't something I condone, but in this case, I wasn't opposed to it. So…school research had suddenly taken on a new, more intimate twist.

Deciding on a pair of navy colored slacks and some matching pumps, I put on a white wrap blouse and some silver and blue jewelry that made it all look a bit more chic than it may have otherwise. After my make-up was on, I appraised myself in the mirror and thought it worked. Interesting and appealing, but not overboard.

Shortly later, I was walking into Beast Company
to announce my presence.

"Charisma Chu for Mason Beast," I said.

The receptionist looked at me and gave me a
slightly scrutinizing gaze, but then announced. "Yes, he's
expecting you, Ms. Chu. Take the elevator to the left and
he's up on the third floor. I'll ring his Executive Assistant
to let her know that you've arrived."

"Thank you," I said.

Standing in the elevator, I looked around. It was
quite the sophisticated looking elevator, more like a
Vegas casino's elevator, than that of a corporate office.
Brass and mirrors and well lit—cameras discreetly tucked
in the corner. Something came over me and I stared into
the camera and smiled. Take that whoever was observing.
Mason, maybe?

"Hello Ms. Chu," I'm Vivian, Mr. Beast's
executive assistant. She extended her hand and I took it

all in. She was perfect—both beautiful and put together in a polished and professional way—no tacky women for Mason.

"Hi Vivian. Please, call me Charisma."

She smiled and nodded. "Mr. Beast is expecting you; follow me."

I walked into Mason's office and immediately loved its musky scent and masculine feel. It was like a law office—organized and precise.

"Charisma, good morning," Mason said. I watched him peruse me from head to toe unapologetically and when our eyes finally connected, I saw approval in his.

"Good morning, Mason. Once again, I wanted to thank you for this opportunity," I said, suddenly feeling a small flip in my stomach. I was nervous! *This is just business*, I thought. *Business excites me; it doesn't make me nervous.*

"Why don't you have a seat," Mason said.

I sat down in one of the black leather chairs and Vivian sat down in the next one.

"This morning I have a few things that have come up and Vivian is going to take you around and introduce you to everyone for me," Mason said in a matter-of-fact voice. I had to admit, his CEO voice was sexy. I also had to admit that I was ridiculously disappointed that Mason wouldn't be taking me around. Why I would have thought he'd book out his entire day for me was ridiculous.

"Wonderful," I said.

"Then we'll go for lunch, say 1:30," Mason said. "If that works, of course."

"That would be fine," I said. Darn, I wish I'd eaten a bit more breakfast. That was a late lunch.

"Okay, that should do it. Vivian, you can follow the agenda I put together earlier," Mason said.

"Yes, Mr. Beast," she said. She got up in a graceful move and walked toward the door, turning around and waiting for me. "Ready?"

"I am," I said. "I just have to grab my portfolio."

Vivian and I walked around and I was introduced to all the key people on the management team in marketing, distribution, legal, accounting, and customer service. Each of them was given one specific set of instructions by Vivian: "Mr. Beast requests that you give Ms. Chu your full cooperation."

It seemed strange telling people to cooperate with me. Usually, they did all on their own and I didn't want people to think I was being a disruption to their day, someone that was there to take up their time more than learn from their experiences.

Before I knew it, it was 1:30 and time to meet Mason for lunch. The time had gone by quickly, but I was so hungry, too. Vivian went one direction and I went to knock on Mason's office door softly, just in case he was on his telephone.

"Come in," I heard a muffled voice say.

I walked in and froze. There he was, changing into his suit from some work-out clothes. His white shirt was open as he pulled on his slacks. I could not stop staring at his tanned and smooth muscular chest. Underneath that suit was one hell of a sexy beast. Pun intended. I almost swallowed my tongue forgetting it was there as I tried not to drool. He was built just as or even more muscular than his underwear model brother. "Sorry, I thought you said to come in."

"I did, no worries," he said confidently, giving me a sly grin. Even that look he gave me…almost predatory and dark sent a chill up my spine. It seemed Mason wasn't just the uptight heir to the Beast throne. He had another side to him.

"Oh." Excessive modestly sure wasn't an issue with him. And from the looks of it, I could see why. He was pretty hot without his clothes on, and he probably knew it.

"Ready for some chocolate cake today?" he asked me, smiling as he buttoned up his white shirt hiding his hot body and put his tie on and then his custom made Italian slate gray suit jacket. With a body like his, his suit couldn't help but look fabulous on him. He could be a cosmetics model or one of those exquisite male cologne models.

"That sounds wonderful," I said, still thinking about that vision of him getting changed.

"Great, there's something that I need to discuss with you," he said. He looked at me and I tried to read what it might be, but I couldn't gauge it. He was as good at showing what he was thinking as he was at hiding it. The perfect poker face.

He told me as soon as we got to the restaurant.

***

"So Charisma, how did your morning go?" Mason
asked right after we sat down at the restaurant at a small
table in the back corner.

"Wonderful. Everyone was nice. I want to make
sure they understand that I'm not here to disrupt their
days, rather to learn from them, though."

"Did anyone give you a hard time?" he asked,
leaning in and raising one eye brow in a speculative way.

"No, nothing like that, Mason. They were all very
polite, but I know how busy people are. It takes a lot to
run a corporation," I said.

"No one really understands that unless they're in
the culture, do they?" Mason said, staring at me, his green
eyes growing slightly darker.

"Not too often. That's the case with even the professors at USC, don't you think?"

Then together we said, "Never worked in a corporate environment." It made us both start laughing.

"Well, we're already finishing each other's sentences," Mason said softly.

I looked at him and was taken aback by the intimate sound of his statement, but I couldn't deny it. It had just happened. "Great minds think alike," I said casually, trying to avoid the fluttering of my nerves under my skin. "So, what was it that you wanted to talk with me about?"

The waitress came up right when I asked that and Mason raised his pointer finger in that "wait a few seconds" look. Then we ordered and he got right back to the question without skipping a beat. "I'm hoping you'll be my guest to an event I have."

"Well, when is it?" I asked. Yes, I was curious and certainly not opposed.

"It's a gala, tonight."

"Tonight?" I asked. That wasn't much time. Galas were big deals, not like a burger after work in your jeans.

"What's it for?" I asked. "That's not much notice."

"Sorry about that, I just remembered it, myself. It's for my fraternity and our annual fundraiser for our cause—childhood hunger. With so much going on, it..." He didn't finish his thought and I didn't need him to, either.

"That's okay, but I don't know, Mason. Not to be cliché, but I don't think I have anything to wear and I have a paper to work on for school." Suddenly I could hear my mother's voice cautioning me, too. Mason was a smooth operator and it wouldn't be wise to let my guards down too quickly—just in case.

"You don't want the kids to go hungry, do you?" he asked.

"Ouch, that's some guilt trip," I said, a coy smile spreading across my face.

"I'll take care of it, Charisma, I assure you."

"And how can you do that?" I asked curiously.

"Well, I took the liberty of picking out a dress that I believe would be perfect for you. It's being delivered to the office right now."

"But after work, I don't know that I'd even have time."

"I can get a stylist up to take care of everything."

"My heels are navy," I protested.

"And Beast Stores has one of the most amazing shoe departments. I believe you've heard of that. And our new cosmetics line, Helen Chu—it's divine."

"I've got make-up covered," I said with a laugh. "But seriously, you can't find anyone else to go."

"I could," he answered directly, but offered nothing more.

"You are certainly persistent, and organized. I think I've run out of excuses to say no," I said. "But, I'd better let Mom know."

"Of course," Mason said. Then he looked down and pinched his fingers on the table cloth, like he was picking up a piece of lint. "Can I be honest with you, Charisma? I'm not really prone to beating around the bush."

"Yes," I said. My heart started racing. To be honest was a vague statement, for certain.

"I was looking for an opportunity to ask you out and this one seems perfect."

"Oh," I gulped. I hadn't expected such a straight forward statement. Despite seeming poised, I was no pro when it came to dating and men. "I'm flattered," I finally sputtered.

"Good, so it's a yes and it's a go?"

"It is," I said.

"For the record, you wouldn't have to change a thing. You're great right now and would more than represent," he said.

"Thank you," I said, my voice barely above a whisper.

***

Back at the office, I called Mom to fill her in. She was so funny, reminding me that I was an adult and didn't have to clear everything through her. Yet, I knew she was grateful that I did call so she wouldn't have to worry. Then she ended with, "Don't do anything you'll regret," which made me laugh.

"Oh Mom, I forgot to ask. Do you need me to come in tomorrow?"

"Thanks for bringing that up. Yes, I do need you, if it works out okay. We have a new employee—some big retail guy who's going to help us integrate our line into Beast Stores—but he doesn't know much about our products so he'll need some guidance. You'd be perfect to do that. Might even learn something for your school paper, too."

"Where'd you find him?" I asked.

"He was recommended through an old friend," she said. I knew she was being vague and it made me curious. When she was that way, it was always something interesting—and something I'd have to wait and see firsthand.

"Okay, so I'll behave tonight so I have a fresh mind," I teased.

"You know, Charisma, I think that Mason has more in mind than just helping you with research on your paper," she said.

"I know—be alert. I will, Mom."

"But have fun, too. You're young and there's more to life than studying and work."

"Spoken by the woman who loves to work," I said.

"Work is my lover," Mom said, making us both laugh.

"Well, the only lover I need is work right now, myself, Mom. Trust me."

"The heart and mind don't always work in unison, my dear."

"On that note, I've got to go," I said.

***

I'd never had a fashion team before, but that's what it felt like as I sat there and let everyone do their magic on me. The dress that Mason had picked was indeed amazing—black with encrusted diamonds and a pair of strappy Manolo Blahnik sandals to match.

Now it was time to get my hair done by Jerry, the stylist.

"You're scrumptious," he said, clapping his hands together. "This will hardly seem like work at all."

"That's nice to say," I said, laughing.

Then Jerry started talking and styling.

"Oh, you're going to look like a movie star," he said.

"And that's not overdoing it for some frat gala?" I asked.

"Don't be silly, chile'. Flaunt it," he replied. "Mason is going to eat you up looking like this, girlfriend. You'll land yourself one of the most sought after bachelors in the world."

"You're mistaken," I said quickly. "I'm not here to land Mason. Furthest thing from my mind."

"Why not? He's clearly into you. He never asks women out to public events—never."

"How do you know?"

"I've been connected with the Beast's for all their events. I know," Jerry said.

"Well, you're wrong on this one," I said defiantly.

He wasn't listening. "Saving yourself for the other brother? Callum? He's a dish…well, he was before that accident. I was a Callum fan before, but now he's pretty pathetic. But Mason, he's looking better every day, honey."

"Um, Jerry, Callum is not even mildly attractive to me. He's rude and arrogant, completely offensive to both me and my mother. In fact, I'd be likely to slap him if I ever see him again. At least he isn't around here while I'm doing my project."

"That one lasted a long time in the news," Jerry said. "That's part of what makes him so pathetic now. Not sure how anyone could come back from that." Then Jerry put a diamond clip securely into my hair, making me flinch for a second as the tines pressed into my scalp. Then he released it and all was well.

As I looked at myself in the mirror, Mason walked into his office, which had been my makeshift beauty central station.

"Wow," Mason said, looking at me with his mouth open. "You are a vision."

Jerry gave me a knowing look and packed up his tools of the trade. "Well, see you girl," he said, kissing each of my cheeks. "And, good luck," he added with a wink.

"I'm not easily impressed, but I am right now. You're wearing the Helen Chu Cosmetics, and they're perfect for the day and equally so for at night. Not that you even need them, of course, because your face is perfect."

His words left me in a state of desire, caution, and excitement. And almost speechless. Before I knew it, we were off to the gala, ready to arrive in his sporty black Jaguar coup.

Chapter 6

Charisma

Mason and his frat brothers were clearly all quite successful. I was shocked to see that their gala was being held at the Beverly Hills Polo Club. Shouldn't have been, I suppose, but I was. If any of them were half as successful as Mason, whether they were from old money or not, it was likely going to be a room filled with influential people. And all I was aware of was Mason and I. It was strange to feel such a draw to him, but I did. What we had in common excited me, plus, he was gorgeous and complimentary. By every outward appearance, he was the complete package.

"So, are you close with all these guys?" I asked Mason, glancing around at all the dressed up men with ornately made-up women by their sides.

"No, not really. We're business close. Callum's really who they are all tight with."

"Do they know the same Callum I met?" I asked jokingly.

Mason looked at me with an appreciative smile. "They do, but they like that type of thing."

"So, Callum paved the way for you to get in. Isn't that how this brotherhood stuff works?"

"Charisma, you'd think it was that simple. They wanted him right away and were pretty unprecedented in their pursuit to get him to pledge back in the day. When I enrolled at USC for undergrad, I naturally chose this option, referred by my big brother and all, but it was a hell of a lot harder for me. At first, anyway."

"At first? Sounds like an interesting story behind it." I said.

Mason shrugged in a casual manner. "Within a year, I became the President and really helped to put a lot of guys on the map, I suppose, focusing on them getting noticed by the right organizations down the line for work, connecting them with alumni that were significant in their fields, that kind of thing. As it turned out, Callum really was only good at being the face of the party boy and kind of a poster child—nothing too serious when all was said and done."

"This may sound harsh, considering all that's happened, but wasn't that basically what he was for Beast Company, too?"

"Not harsh, and you're right, but Father was constantly trying to get him to change it up. He just didn't grasp it, or didn't want to, anyway."

"So, Mason, who is this exquisite beauty?" some guy said, walking up to us. He spoke with his jaw clenched and still managed to show a pearly white smile. Kind of creepy, to me, anyway.

"Samuel, let me introduce Charisma Chu," Mason said. He grabbed my arm gently and said, "Charisma, this is Samuel Johnson."

"It's nice to meet you, Samuel," I said, extending my hand. He grabbed it and then handed his drink to the woman he was with to cup his other hand over mine.

Gross and rude, dude.   Keep your hands to yourself.

I pulled it away and smiled and then introduced myself to the lady he was with. It was his girlfriend, it turned out.

"So, have you two been dating long?" Samuel asked.

I didn't know what to say, but it turned out that I didn't need to say a word. Mason was more than glad to answer, "Not too long." I smiled at the mysterious smile on his face. He could have said we were engaged if it protected me from this Samuel joker hitting on me or acting so creepy.

"You'd better grab her quick, Mason, or I might just take her," Samuel said.

That was so rude. I looked at the woman next to him and she didn't seem to care. I had friends like her—she was settling, which was sad. No one should settle. "Well Samuel, you can't grab me if I can run faster."

He was shocked and then laughed, calling me a firecracker.

"Mason, will you take me over there to get me another glass of wine," I said, batting my eyes.

"Of course," he said. He turned to Samuel. "If you'll excuse us."

No sooner were we walking away than he was laughing. "You're good."

"I hope I didn't embarrass you. I can't stand guys like that," I said.

"No, you actually made my night. That was good, certainly out of the norm for Samuel," Mason said.

After getting our drinks, we just stood in the corner talking and occasionally talking to someone that would invade our bubble, but I had the distinct feeling that Mason wanted people to see me, not talk to me. He wanted me all to himself, and it was kind of endearing. Maybe a bit possessive, but it didn't seem like it was for bad intentions. Plus, if these other guys were a lot like that Samuel, I was glad to keep my distance.

Mason reached over to me and grabbed my wine glass. "Care to dance?"

"I'd love to," I said, smiling at him.

Hand in hand, Mason guided us toward the dance floor and turned around, pulling me into his arms in a graceful manner. His hand was pressed firmly against my lower back and our bodies were so close that I could feel his heart's beat. It was so soothing and I felt really safe and aroused by our close connection.

"You're driving these guys crazy. They can't keep their eyes off you," Mason said to me.

"And how would you know, Mr. Beast. You aren't taking your eyes off me, either."

He smiled and leaned in. I thought he was going to kiss me but he went to the left of my head and right to my ear.

With a soft whisper that tickled my skin, he said, "You truly are exquisite. Unlike anyone I've ever laid eyes upon before."

"Are all the Beast men so charming?" I asked.

"I think you know that isn't the case," Mason said with a crooked smile. "But those of us who honor our family do try our best."

"What do you mean?" I asked. That was a curious and intriguing statement.

"There is a lot of pride by most of us in the Beast name and legacy. I love the business and from the time I was fifteen, I dove into it, eager to learn everything I could and excited about the potential of continuing on in excellence, as both my father and grandfather did."

I watched his lips as he spoke and felt empowered by his words. "I understand," I said. "We're not from old money, like you, but I'd do anything for my mother and the business. She's worked hard and I want her to be proud of me in all that I do."

"I am pretty sure you've succeeded. Your mother is highly respected, and I can already tell that you are, too."

"Now those are words to sweep a woman off her feet," I said in a merry laugh. It was such an intimate conversation and the way that his hand made my lower back tingle had me discombobulated. I wanted to talk and talk, but I also wanted to…well, I couldn't let my mind go there. It was far too soon to have thoughts like that.

"What do you say we go? I promised you that I'd get you back to the office early tonight and I don't want to back out, or else you may never agree to go anywhere with me again," Mason said.

I was having so much fun, but Mason was right.

"Okay then, so long as you think you've made your presence for long enough," I said.

"I think they'll understand. It's really about the money, anyway, nothing more."

***

Mason and I were standing side by side, looking out of his office window at the beautiful Newport Beach city below us, the ocean off in the distance, barely visible by the bright white of the full moon that was out. Maybe it was the moon or maybe the amazing evening, but for the first time in a long time, school work was far from my mind.

"This really is a special view," I said. "You're fortunate."

"I count my blessings every day, of course, but more than fortunate, it's hard work that gets someone here. I have no doubts that you'll have just such a view at some point in the future."

"Maybe from this office," I teased.

"A Chu invasion of Beast Company. I can't say that I'm opposed to it," Mason said. Then his hand reached under my chin and he softly turned my face toward his and leaned in and kissed me.

His lips were urgent and gentle as they brushed against mine. I gladly responded, taking in the feelings of the moment and realizing that it felt absolutely perfect.

"Is this okay?" he finally asked, pulling slightly away from me.

I nodded my head down, not certain if I could talk. Then he leaned in again and kissed me harder, wrapping his arms around me. They didn't move, only holding me tightly as we kept kissing. I was surprised at how receptive I was to it, how much I wanted it.

Again, Mason pulled back and put one of his hands on each side of my face and leaned in closer to me. In a soft voice he spoke while staring me right in the eyes. "I know that we've only really known each other for a few days, but I can't stop thinking of you, Charisma. Even on that night, I was so drawn to you that it drove me crazy."

"I feel the same way," I said. It was true; I thought about him a lot.

It was only when he said, "I think I'm falling for you," that I got scared. What did that mean? And how could it be? That was too quick. But my fears subsided by another kiss and when I finally left Beast Company that night, I could feel his kiss lingering on my lips for the entire ride home. Even after I showered, his presence was

still there, somehow becoming a part of me from just a
single night.

Chapter 7

<u>Charisma</u>

If my school work topic the night before had been on the perfect kiss, I would have nailed it. But as fate would have it, it wasn't and that made it an impossible endeavor. I ended up drifting off to sleep with thoughts of Mason's scrumptious lips on mine and I woke up with that thought still there. I was dreamy and had a permanent smile. I didn't think anything would be able to wipe it off my face, either. Was there such a thing as an after-kiss glow? If there was, I got it. Hey, after-kiss glow would be a great name for a lipstick color, too. I'd have to remember that.

Driving out to Costa Mesa where I was to meet my mother at the factory, I thought about Mason the man. I loved it that he placed such high priorities on work and family. Having always been just Mom and me, I'd always wanted to have more of a family, but talking with Mason made me realize that it came with its challenges, too.

And what a gentleman he was, too. Funny how two guys could be raised in the same environment and turn out so differently. I had no doubts that Callum Beast never had been and never could be a gentleman. Too self-absorbed and arrogant for that. Probably still was, deformity and all. But enough about him. Why bother when I can think about Mason?

"Hi Charisma, you look happy today," Jenna said. She was the greeter at the factory, the one who signed people in and handed out visitor passes, things like that.

"I am happy, Jenna."

"Must have been a good night," she said with a sweet smile.

I just winked and kept on walking. Let everyone wonder. I didn't mind.

I walked over to my desk and put my things down
and then picked up the phone to buzz my mother. She'd
been at the factory since 6 AM, just like she was most
every day.

"Charisma, hi, did you have a good night?"

"It was great," I said.

"Wonderful. Now, come to my office. Our new
employee is here and waiting for you to show the ropes."

"Okay," I said. After she hung up, I couldn't help
but notice how strange it was that she didn't ask any other
questions. It was not like my mother. Maybe she was
reserved because of the new employee. That must be it.

It didn't take long for me to find out why, and it
was quite a shock.

***

"Hi," I said and I froze. *No, not today*, I thought.

"Charisma, you remember Callum Beast, I assume," my mother said.

"Yes," I managed to blurt. "But what is he doing here, in your office?"

"He's our new employee," my mother said. She was smiling, a bit amused and very controlled. I had to blink to make sure I wasn't hallucinating. Nope—this was real.

I looked at Mother and then at Callum. It was the first time I'd seen him and the stories about what happened to his appearance were not at all far-fetched. That accident had really altered him. He barely resembled the man from the party and the timid look on his face was almost heartbreaking. And I emphasize almost. But there he was, eating humble pie at the very place he called "cheap."

"Callum, Charisma will show you all the ropes and give you an overview of everything. She knows just as much as I do, maybe more. I'm sure you'll get a grasp of it quickly, you've grown up in a world that understands the importance of the cosmetics industry."

I remained quiet while I listened to Mother talk. She could have been having some fun taking revenge on him for what he'd done, but she wasn't. I should have known she wouldn't; she was too good of a woman. Instead of spite, she treated him with respect and kindness like she did all the company's employees and everyone in general. That was her, not me. I wasn't so quick to be that kind.

After Mother had finished what she had to say, Callum and I went back to my office. I opened the door and walked in, standing by it until he passed, and then shut the door behind me.

"Have a seat," I said.

He sat down in the red chair that was on the other side of my desk and I walked around to the other side of my desk, but didn't sit. I stood there and looked at him.

Adrenaline started to run through me and it made me feel like shaking, but I controlled it.

"Is this some kind of joke? Did you not have enough fun humiliating my mom and this place at the Beast Company party? Why are you here? What do you intend to do? Steal our formula and expose any secrets you think we may have? See if we really make knock offs and cheap Made in Chu crap? Please, go home and play with your floozies. We run a legitimate hard-working business here, and we don't have time for your stupid little games." I knew there was no way he could answer all those questions and that I'd just completely unleashed on him, but I didn't care. I didn't have any trust for him and I was going to make sure he damn well knew it.

That was when Callum sat back down in his chair, bent over and began shaking. What? Was this some kind of ploy?

I didn't walk around my desk, but did call out. "Are you okay?"

He just shook.

When I'd said those things, I'd expected him to fight back and come up with some hateful words that would prove I was right. Instead, there he was, looking weak and timid. Pathetic, really. Now I felt bad. So help me, if he was yanking my chain, I'd deliver him that slap I said I wanted to just yesterday.

"Hey what's going on?" I cautiously asked, walking around the desk and kneeling down to check on him. "Why are you shaking like that?"

He didn't answer.

I asked again, but when he looked up, I saw that his eyes were filled with tears, his long lashes wet from crying. Tracks of tears were streaming down his face and he looked so broken that I felt my throat constricting to not cry myself. *Stop it, he doesn't need pity*, I thought.

"Callum, just tell me what's wrong," I said, standing back up and giving him some space. I felt awkward now and like I was the one who was a real jackass.

"Can't you see?" he said, his teeth gritted together in a look of obvious excruciating pain. "Everything is wrong! I'm sorry for everything I've caused because of my stupidity. I don't know how I'll ever make it up to you, your mother, everyone. And my father, I can't make it up to him. He's dead and died humiliated because of me. The only way I can think of to try and make it better is to hope that through my actions, your mother and you can someday forgive me. I didn't know how to do that without coming here."

"Mom said you were recommended by a friend, and she said you were the help she needed, but…"

"She put me to work right when I visited, told me she needed extra help because you had stuff to do, and put me to work right away," Callum said.

"Well, that's my mom for you. She has a heart of gold," I said. I felt bad about this situation and even pitied

Callum, but that wasn't what he needed. And I was not willing to give him a free pass. I'd be respectable, but certainly not do anything to become closer to him, either. "I know that you aren't ready to take over CEO at Beast, but why not do something else there?"

"I don't know what I'd do there, either. I'm not fit for ad campaigns anymore. Mason is running things now, and I'm just not...just not needed."

"Well, you must be set up well enough that you could do something educational while you are getting back into the swing of things," I offered.

"No, I don't have anywhere to go. This is it," Callum said.

"I'm no following. What do you mean, exactly?"

"Well, my penthouse is company owned and run through the business, so I'm out. They're using it as a corporate apartment for the managers of our overseas locations when they come for meetings."

"And your family home?"

"It's embarrassing to say it, but I've burnt so many bridges, been such a prick to so many people that they don't really want me there, either."

"That's horrible!" I exclaimed.

"It's true. But worst of all, I have a hard time even looking my mom in the eyes. She loves me, I know, but I basically killed the love of her life." He began trembling again and I felt so bad about it. This really was some crazy karma that had come Callum's way, very hard for me to imagine.

"And you can't live with Mason?" I asked.

"No." He didn't elaborate any further on Mason. "That's why I am so thankful to your mother. She said your place was big enough that I could stay there while I rebuild myself. Without her kindness...I just don't know."

"Excuse me, I don't think I heard you correctly, Callum." He was clearly upset enough that he wasn't making any sense. "Where are you staying?"

"At your place," he said.

I had heard him right, and I was in shock. Why would Mom invite this hateful ass to live in our home, our sanctuary? Down on his luck or not, he had to have someone else he could stay with. "You're kidding, right?" Lame question, but the best I could do.

"No, I'm not. Wish I were. None of my friends would help me out, either. I asked, which was hard to do, but it was pretty damn easy for them to say 'no' to me."

I couldn't believe all of this and tried to put it out of my mind. I kept shoving Callum off on various people to explain their roles and doing what I needed to do. Every time I saw him I felt like I might be having a nightmare too. The entire situation sucked in my opinion. But I kept busy. The reality of it hit home when Mom entered into my office and said, "Charisma, why don't you take Callum home and give him the guest room. Make sure he has everything he needs, okay?"

"Okay," I said. I didn't want to, but I would never disrespect my mother by questioning her decision, especially in front of *him*.

Once in my car, just having him there next to me was unsettling. We pulled up and I went into the garage with my car and we walked into the house through the service door. "I'm sure this is much smaller than what you're used to, Callum."

"I don't care," he said.

Admittedly, I was slightly impressed that he'd managed to hold his tongue from the darkness that was likely still in his heart all day. I'd never let him know that, though.

I showed him around to where all the pertinent things he'd need was, avoiding Mom and my bedrooms, and then took him to the guest suite on the opposite side of the house where his room would be. When we walked into it I saw that all his things were already there. Mom definitely didn't waste any time.

Callum looked over at me and even though I stared at him with callous disregard, I could see that something was in his eyes that couldn't be avoided. It was different and softer than what I'd noticed the first time I met him, or even when he'd spent time together today. It was gratitude. And seeing it on his face made him seem like a different person—a tolerable person, at least. Maybe he was just a broken guy who needed saving. Just so long as my mom did the saving for Callum Beast we'd be fine, because it was not a job that I was interested in.

Chapter 8

Charisma

Having Callum at my smaller sized casa was awful. I couldn't stand it that I could be sitting in my room with the door open or trying to do some work in the living room and I'd see him. I tried to avoid him, but inevitably my luck always ran out and I'd see him. And his body, it was so strange. From a distance, it was beautiful despite losing a bit of its definition due to him not being able to work out, but up close, it was so scarred up, along with his face, that I felt like a piece of scum because the name Frankenstein would often cross my mind.

I was sitting by the table, working on my paper for Beast Company, and enjoying a glass of much needed red wine to help me wind down. It had been a long and taxing day, one in which I received bad news that some of our shipments for new ingredients was delayed in customs at some port in France. Having production fall behind was not ideal and that was just what was going to happen if it didn't get cleared up pronto.

"You okay?" Callum asked, walking up to me. He had on a pair of shorts and was holding a t-shirt in his hand.

I looked up at him and couldn't help it, but my eyes went to the L shaped scar on his chest. He noticed and quickly put his shirt on, suddenly embarrassed, which made me embarrassed, too. "Sorry, you didn't have to do that. I just noticed it," I said softly.

"I can't stand looking at those scars. I don't expect any differently from anyone else, Charisma."

"The sooner you accept it, the happier you'd be, yes?" I asked.

"I suppose, but I'm not here to talk about scars." His voice was terse.

"What did you need?" I asked, glancing into his eyes. They were always so charged with emotion now— emotions that I didn't really understand.

"I was just wondering what was on our schedule tomorrow?" he asked.

"You'll be with Wanda in Product Development. It's may day over at Beast Company," I said. I felt bad saying it, but he knew I went there and it was the truth, so...

"Oh, got it," he said.

"Do you ever visit over there?" I asked.

"No, just too painful," he said to me.

"And how about your mother? Have you seen her lately?"

"We met for lunch, but I feel so strange being out in public. People look, but that's not so bad. They talk, too, and while I don't care what they say about me, Charisma, I care about how they look at me. My last name has never seemed so cliché before."

I laughed softly. "I can see how that might sting you a bit, but Callum, I think there's an opportunity in all of this that will be good. Even if you don't know what it is yet, I think it'll happen."

For a moment, we just looked at each other and I couldn't help but get philosophical. What was the price someone had to pay for their mistakes? Callum's had been high, no doubt, and even though I'd held plenty of resentment toward him for the way he'd acted, I was beginning to feel that he'd paid the price. Things couldn't get much worse for the guy.

"Hey, tomorrow night a bunch of us are getting together for a few drinks after work. Would you be interested in joining us?" I asked.

Callum looked excited and then it was quickly replaced with a bit of panic and fear. "That sounds good, but probably not a good idea. I'm not supposed to drink, not sure I'd be strong enough to not be tempted to."

"I'm sorry, Callum. I keep forgetting…" I didn't know what else to say. I'd been trying to be nice, but I felt like I'd just been really insensitive.

"Don't be sorry. The rest of the world doesn't need to stop living while I figure things out," he said.

"My mother is rubbing off on you," I said.

"What do you mean?" he asked.

"That just sounds like something she'd say, that's all. All the ancient Chinese proverbs that she incorporates in a modern way. That kind of thing."

"I've grown to like those," Callum confessed. "It's like a walking, talking calendar with the thought for the day.

I burst out into laughter. "That is so true."

Through laughter, I felt myself drawn more to Callum. He did have a sense of humor behind it all and a witty intelligence. Maybe he'd start showing it more. From my perspective, that would definitely be a gift. The world deserved to see his best potential, after all.

We were both silent for a bit and I finally said, "Well, I've got to get back to work on this now. Can't believe how fast the deadline's approaching."

"Good night then," Callum said.

"Good night," I said. He turned to walk away and I noticed how he really did look like a manly man. It was intriguing, but why? He certainly wasn't my type—not like Mason was.

***

It had been hard to stop thinking about the frat gala and the great connection that Mason and I had that evening. Work had been busy that week and while it had just been five days ago, it felt like an eternity. More than I wanted to admit, I was hoping that Mason would ask me out again. But my common sense would take over and I'd think, *at least stay low until your project with the company is over and see what happens from there.*

So, oddly enough despite it all, I found myself spending a lot more time with Callum these days at the cosmetics company over Mason at Beast. We were on our way over to the marketing department to view some sketches and concepts for the Christmas launch, which was crazy. I guess that's how Christmas in July and concepts like that were born, because the holidays seemed like an eternity away.

"What do you think of the industry so far? Is it as boring and cheap as you'd envisioned?" I asked, half sarcastically.

"You don't want to let me live that down, do you? I don't blame you, I guess," Callum said.

I breathed in deeply. "Callum, stop. I'm not saying it to be mean, just so we can have a good laugh about it. It's taken a lot to be able to get over it and laugh about it so it shows we've come a long way. Also, I want to get past the past and get the tension out of the way. I mean how else are we going to work and live together if we don't?"

"Sorry, just a habit I've gotten. I cannot stop beating myself up," he said.

"I get that, really I do." I put my hand on his shoulder and rubbed it softly. "We've all had those moments. Maybe you should go talk with someone about it, someone who is better in that area of expertise than I ever will be."

"Like your mom?" he asked.

"While she is a wealth of wisdom, I was thinking of someone you don't know. Like a therapist, maybe. You have all these things you're trying to change so quickly and maybe they can help you recognize just how much you've grown already."

"You think I've grown?" he asked.

I looked into his eyes that were loaded with hope. Did I think he'd grown? "I'm not sure I can answer that. I don't know what's inside of you, but I think you have."

"Why?"

"Well Callum, when I first saw you I was so angry at you, I never felt so much hate for anyone. It was hard to be around you, because what you said was very hurtful. Being hated on, especially for no reasons, is unfair and unforgiveable; it made me filled with hate towards you as well. And it didn't feel good being this hateful, too.

But I think fate had punished you enough. I think you're sincere about being sorry and wanting to change. It's just been a few short days but we've spent a ton of time together, that I don't feel angry towards you anymore. It's unhealthy for both of us. So, through me

changing my perspective, I think it's only natural that
you've changed too."

"Thanks, that means the world coming from you.
I really am trying, but I'm not a therapist type of guy. If I
can't do this on my own, it is not worth doing."

"Now that is a Beast trait that I recognize," I said
with a smile. He sounded like Mason just now.

"As it turns out, I'm not going to be going out for
drinks tonight. I was wondering if you wanted to go catch
an art exhibit that one of my old prep school friends is
having at a small gallery in Malibu tonight. Should be
fun—nothing fancy. Early night." I offered this, hoping it
didn't sound like a date, because it was meant as a gesture
of friendship.

"I'd like that," he said.

"Excellent. Well, here we are," I said, looking at
the board room. I loved that room. It was very modern
and trendy, having lilac themed décor all around it with

rich chestnut wood. It was feminine, yes, but also quite masculine in its own unique way.

***

It didn't take a lot of days to pass by for Callum and me to fall into a routine that involved being more comfortable around each other. It was normal and I no longer waited for that zing about him catching me in my sweatpants or wearing no make-up. And during the days I was at the cosmetics company, he became my sidekick. We were everywhere together and the awkward moments were less, the good conversation moments more.

Chapter 9

<u>Charisma</u>

All the relaxation that had come between Callum
and me in a relatively quick period of time had turned into
anxiety with Mason. Maybe it was underlying
expectations based on that amazing night and the way he
kissed me, or our ambitions, which wouldn't settle for
anything less than being professional around the office
environment. Mason needed to be that way because he
was the acting CEO. I wanted to be that way, because I
didn't want anyone to discredit my intelligence as I did
research for my paper. It was my brain that had gotten me
there, not some pending relationship with Mason. So,
despite what my heart was interested in, I fought it with
my intellect and kept things quite casual on a personal
level. I didn't know how else I could achieve what I
wanted.

"Hey, you look great today," Mason said, looking at me.

"Thanks," I said.

"How's the paper coming along? Need any of my time today?" he asked.

"Initially, I did, but I actually was able to tap into the answers I needed, so no, I'm good."

"Oh," he said. I think he was disappointed.

And so it went on. The two of us did a nervous dance around each other, but hands down, Mason was more nervous than me. I kept thinking of how he said he was falling for me that night and assumed it was in the heat of the moment. He hadn't known me long enough to fall in love with me, right?

My day moved forward and we passed each other in the halls occasionally, giving a friendly hello and smile. At the end of that day, I went back to my small make-shift office in a smaller conference room that Mason had set up for me and started to collect my things to head home for the day.

On the table was a small silver box that was tied with a deep blue bow. I wondered what it was, but not who it was from. "Mason," I said.

"You called," he answered.

I just about jumped out of my skin. "You scared me!"

"Sorry, didn't mean to. I just wanted to see your reaction when you opened it."

"Okay then," I said, smiling at him and walking over to the box. It was beautiful and barely bigger than a ring box. There was no way it would be that, though.

I slowly released the bow of the blue ribbon and set it on the table and lifted up the lid of the box, so curious about its contents. When I saw it my eyes popped open. I slowly lifted up a chain and at the end of it was a pewter turtle. Definitely interesting…certainly nothing I would have guessed.

"This is great, thank you," I said.

"Do you know what the turtle symbolizes?" he asked.

"No, what?" Now things were getting interesting.

"It's my way of apologizing to you," Mason said. He looked embarrassed and I saw his hands pressed into his pants pockets, nervously fidgeting.

"For what? You don't have anything to apologize for."

"I think I moved a bit too fast the other night when I shared what I did. It wasn't my intention to, trust me, but it just came out. The moment felt right, I guess, but I think it had made you too uncomfortable, and for that, I'm sorry."

"Mason, it's not that, really, but that's sweet. There is just so much on my plate right now, between school, here, and at the cosmetics company. I want to give each my best effort."

"Which doesn't leave room for any fun for you?" he asked dejectedly.

"Not much, but the fun will come after the hard work."

"Does your mother say that, Charisma?"

"Actually no," I said with a little laugh, "she's always reminding me that I'm young and need to have some fun too."

"Well, if you ever take her advice keep me in mind." Then he walked out, leaving me with a confused smile on my face and warmth in my heart that I couldn't deny. What the turtle symbolized was really endearing.

Which led to a gift the next day, a song send to my email from some country group that I never would have known—Zac Brown Band—and the song *Keep me in Mind.* He was clever and I liked that he had ideas that didn't just involve spending money, they came from his heart.

For the next week, every other day when I was at Beast Company, Mason had some clever thing to offer me. One day it was a chair massage complimentary of this amazing woman, Gina, who traveled around to businesses and offered them. I loved it and definitely thought she would be welcome at Helen Chu Cosmetics, too. The next day it was a new portfolio with my monogram. Then there was a single flower—a Stargazer Lily—which happened to be the name of the shade of lipstick I'd worn that day. His gifts were thoughtful, and showed he really wanted to know more about me.

At the end of the week, Mason came and knocked on my door as I was preparing to leave Beast that day. "Okay, I know that you don't have to work on your paper this weekend, and that you've had a long week, which is why I'd like to take you out to a movie and dinner tonight. Casual—jeans and fun—nothing serious or exhausting, I promise." He held up his hand like he was taking the Hippocratic Oath.

"I surrender," I said, raising my arms. "Where can I meet you?"

"I'll pick you up at your home. Friday night traffic is hardly relaxing for a driver, is it?"

"Good point," I said. "7:00?"

"Perfect," Mason said, smiling a gorgeous smile that lit up his entire face as he walked out. It would be a miracle if I could stay casual with him tonight. His smile sent goosebumps up my arm as I noticed how he was becoming more and more handsome as he began losing more of his business-like mask and letting his more authentic self out, like moments as this one. His gifts over the past week showed that he was also a sensitive and deep person. Despite his riches, he was a man of substance. He also cherished what he had and didn't take the hard work his ancestors did for him to enjoy his life today. Unlike the old Callum did. I reached for the turtle pendant which was tucked under my blouse for that day and felt it, smiling brightly myself.

I was looking forward to my date with Mason and ready to take the next step further in our relationship but was somehow nervous. It made no sense at all but I didn't want Callum seeing Mason pick me up. Let alone date me. Although we were now just friends and it shouldn't matter, I didn't want his feelings hurt by it. Maybe I was just sensitive to Callum's feelings of betrayal and guilt from his family or maybe it was something else?

Chapter 10

Callum

I'd changed so much since the accident.
Outwardly, this change was obvious. I was no longer an
attractive man and I had to accept that. But no one could
have been more surprised than me to discover that it could
happen relatively quickly and with the help of the two
women that had led to the entire thing unfolding. Helen
Chu was an amazing woman, one of those who were filled
with grace and tenacity that you usually only read
about—never had a chance to meet or be on the receiving
end of it. Now that I got to know her, I felt so ashamed
and humbled by what I did to her. She had the elegance
and nobility of a queen. Everything she did reminded me
of those great ladies you could only wish to meet in
history. I've never met anyone classier than her, including
my mother.

How she could even be so gracious to me after all the shameful things I did was testimony to her strength of character. I was eternally grateful to her. But it was Charisma that had really done the most for me as a man, making me realize what the important qualities of being a man were.

Every time I'd walk around the corner late at night to get something from the kitchen, I'd see Charisma at the table, studying so hard and completely focused on her laptop. She always had this same expression—a content look that showed she loved what she was doing and she'd always softly bite her pretty lips, as if it helped her to think. I halfway wondered if there was a dent in those beautiful lips from that habit. If there was, it would only lend to her perfection. By looks alone, she could conquer the world, but she never relied on it, like I did, and she worried more about helping her mother out and doing well in school and at work than anything else, that she never did anything for herself. The entire time I was a Helen Chu's, Charisma didn't take a break or do anything fun. She was the hardest working person I knew besides Mason, Helen, and my father.

Beautiful Girl: Modern Beauty and Beast (Happy Ever After Standalone Novel Series)

She and Helen never complained about working hard, and never seemed bitter about all the adversities they suffered through, including jealous rivals in cosmetics, sabotaging partners, and the backstabbing that can happen in any industry especially when someone small but talented comes along and threatened the status quo of the bigger players. I didn't know how hard it was for a startup like Helen Chu's Cosmetics to become so successful. It opened my eyes to everything, and made me realized how immature and stupid I was to insult them and think I was anything but superior to them or anyone just because my Grandfather became successful, and I was a leech riding on the coattail of his hard work and success. And then ruining the good will he built for the family name.

How could I have been so low? So classless? So ugly? I can't even explain it because I can't even comprehend why I was so full of hatred that I had to take it out on an innocent sweet woman like Helen. Why was I such an insufferable stupid bully? The only thing I can do now is to try to make it up to Helen and Charisma. To the day I die, I will try to fix what I did, as my dad's dying wish.

"Hey, do you like British humor?" I asked softly, not wanting to startle Charisma as I approached her.

"Yeah, I guess, haven't watched much of it," she said, looking up at me over the top of her laptop screen.

"Well, I saw that A&E is playing an old Monte Python classic, The Holy Grail, in a half hour. I'm going to be watching it if you want to join me," I said. *Please join me*, I thought. I hadn't talked to her much that day and a day didn't feel complete without her around me for at least a little bit of time. I missed her. Terribly.

Mason was such a lucky bastard to get her for an entire day at Beast Company when she was there. I doubt he realized it since all he'd think about was the bottom line at Beast's. He was so buried in ledgers and paperwork, he'd wouldn't even notice if the most beautiful woman stood naked in front of him. But then again, he didn't have Charisma in front of him before.

"Sure, I am finishing up on a section of this and then I'll join you for a bit before I get some sleep. It's been a hectic day," she said, smiling at me. I wanted to capture that smile in a photograph or a painting, it was so beautiful. It was full of joy, kindness, playfulness, and appreciation. And it was directed at me. Despite how much I think she must hate me, she seemed to appreciate me, too.

I paused for a minute and realized she was waiting for me to leave so she could get back to work. I gladly did, knowing that the sooner I left, the sooner she'd come by me. Of course, I really never got British humor, but so many of my friends loved it so I thought I'd give it a try. Maybe with this new life perspective, I'd like it just a bit more. And hopefully, I could get it if I wasn't stoned out of my mind like a lot of my friends liked to be when they watched it.

***

Watching quirky guys running along a desolate mountain region while their servant clacked coconuts together to make it sound like they were on horses was surprisingly entertaining. Who would have thought! I laughed at it, but what made me smile most was watching Charisma's expressions as she looked at the silly movie. Her eyes lit up when she was shocked and her hand flopped over her eyes adorably when she was in disbelief. She was so animated and natural about it, not holding back or calculating her every move. She was herself, and she was being it around me. It felt like a major achievement and when I saw that side of her, I couldn't help but realize everything that I'd lost out on over the years by not embracing this type of life. It wasn't boring; it was fulfilling.

Before we both knew it, the credits were rolling and Charisma looked over at the clock. "Oh my gosh, it's so late! I wasn't planning on being up past midnight."

"Sorry about that. Did you like it?"

"It was funny, but I wouldn't need to see it every day, you know. I think that a little can probably go a long way."

"Agreed," I said.

We both stood up and I said, "So, see you in the
morning?"

"In the morning. Want to carpool?" she asked.
Then she started laughing. It had become our joke. Now
that I didn't have a license for awhile, I was completely
reliant on her or her mother to get to work. And I didn't
particularly like going with Helen since she got there at 6
AM, so I only did that every other day when Charisma
went to Beast for the day.

Morning came and I wasn't tired at all, because I
was riding high on the energy of a great night. It was those
little, unsuspecting moments that really got me excited,
and I would never be experiencing them without
Charisma. She made all the difference and showed me
that being authentic and genuine was such a better deal
than keeping up appearances or struggling to be the life
of the party. Being the life of the party had robbed me of
having a life.

With two large cups of piping hot coffee in tow, Charisma and I made our way to the office, talking about everything going on that day at work. I was feeling good and excited about work, but also excited about seeing where this connection with Charisma could take me.

"Hey, did you want to go do something tonight?" I asked as we sat still in the freeway, waiting for an accident to clear up.

"Oh, I can't tonight. Have plans already," she said. She didn't say anything else and I was so curious to know what her plans were. It was ridiculous, of course, because she didn't owe me any explanations about what she was doing any more than I owed her any. But I was a bit lonely, if I were to honestly express it. Since the accident, my friends and I weren't really tight anymore. We'd talk on the phone, but I found out that a share of them weren't really true friends. Hanging out with a monster wasn't a part of their plan. And the ones who didn't care were too into partying and I couldn't risk being by them, either. I was determined to stay away from

drugs and alcohol with my own willpower, not with going
to a support group.

"Got it," I said, smiling. "Maybe another night
then."

"Yeah, maybe," she said, glancing over at me and
then looking straight ahead.

The accident had cleared up and the car ahead of
us wasn't moving, which made Charisma lay on her horn
and call out some comments that I'd never heard her say
before. "That was something," I said, trying to hide my
laugh.

She looked at me with that same frown, but it
quickly turned to a smile. "I've never been good at road
rage. Not believable."

"And let me say that I'm glad," I added.
"Otherwise, I might just walk to work."

"I noticed that you were working out again. How's that going?" Charisma asked me.

"Good, I'm sore but it feels good. Relieves the stress and reminds me that I have way too many muscles I don't use." And that was the topic that took us to work— sharing stories of funny occurrences that happened while working out. The woman could make any topic interesting.

***

Admittedly, I was curious. When Charisma said she was getting picked up that evening for wherever she was going, I made sure that I was in a place where I'd see who it was that was picking her up. A girlfriend or a guy friend—I wanted to know.

From my room, I heard a car pull up into the driveway and I glanced out. My face fell. It was a black Jaguar—Mason's Jaguar. Why was she going out with him? It instantly stung, but I tried to not jump to any conclusions, as tough as that was. *Of course they're probably friends*, I thought. Charisma could make friends very easily so why not Mason?

Mason and I weren't on very good terms yet and he was still plenty mad at me about what had happened. I got that, but I hadn't seen him for a bit so I thought I'd go out and say hi to him, at least.

When I walked out into the living room, Charisma was opening the front door and I saw a bouquet of white roses being handed to her and Mason's head leaning in for a kiss. It made me sick to my stomach and my fists clenched together in rage, a sudden protective feeling coming over me about Charisma. Were they dating? Why wouldn't she say anything about it?

"You look gorgeous. Ready to go?" Mason asked.

Charisma turned around and met my eyes briefly, a flicker of guilt crossing them, and then turned back to Mason. "I'm ready."

Then the two left, leaving me all alone—painfully alone and realizing something that I didn't want. I was in love with Charisma. In a short amount of time, I'd managed to fall in love with someone that made me feel better than any other woman ever had in my life, and we hadn't even kissed or fooled around. That meant it was the real deal, right?

This intense anger went through me at a breakneck speed and I felt this intense desire to destroy something...make that someone—my brother. Mason was a louse and he knew that it would bother me if he came to pick Charisma up at the house. Did she know it, too? Was she not really as nice and authentic as I'd thought? I didn't know, but from where I stood, he was the problem, not her.

Unable to contain my rage, I quickly changed into some running clothes and took off down the sidewalk toward the running path a mile away. I had to get rid of what I was feeling before I had a setback. And, I had to find a way to take Charisma away from Mason. He didn't deserve her, the arrogant prick. He was all business and if she was with him, she'd become that, too.

With each step I ran, my mind kept shouting, "my heart is breaking," over and over. But when I stopped and caught my breath, I began to plan for what I wanted, not what I felt at that moment. I wanted to win Charisma's love. The only way to do that was to show her that I was a smart man, a changed man. Because of what I did and my role in causing the death of my father, the Board practically threw me out on the streets. They kept me away and appointed Mason as the Interim CEO of Beast's, instead of me. I'd gain the Board's trust again at Beast Company and take my rightful spot as CEO, ousting Mason for good.

Chapter 11

Charisma

When we pulled up to the private airport I knew that I was in for quite the evening. When I saw the helicopter with the Beast Company emblem on the side, my suspicions were confirmed.

"Where are we going?" I asked, my eyes wide. I'd never been on a helicopter before.

"To the family home on Catalina Island," Mason said. His smile was flirty and relayed how delighted he was in his surprise. "Come on, you ready?"

"I am, but where's the pilot?"

Mason looked at me and pointed to himself. "At your service. I assure you, you're in good hands, Charisma."

I had no idea if he was talking about flying or something else, but I was intrigued. "Well, I can't wait."

Both of us had on our headphones so we could talk while making the half hour flight to Catalina Island, where he was able to land right on the roof of his family's estate. Honestly, I'd never experienced anything like it before, and it was such a rush that I could see how people got wrapped up in their uber-wealthy lives. I'd better be careful.

"Welcome to Chateau Falaise," Mason said, extending his hand to me so I could get out of the helicopter. The blades were still rotating slowly despite it being turned off and I ducked down cautiously. I was definitely attached to keeping my head attached to the rest of my body.

"This view is so amazing," I said, looking around. I could see small waves below and thought it was the most majestic view—on the cliffs of the Pacific Ocean, the sun slowly starting to set.

"I never get sick of it. I don't get the chance to get out here enough," Mason said.

"Is your mother home?"

"No," he said with a smile. "Do you really think I'd take you here on this date you finally agreed to just so you could hang out with Mother?" He had a crooked grin on his face that made him look entirely too sexy for that moment.

"From that tone, I'm going to go with 'no'," I said.

"Let's go and I'll give you a tour while the chef prepares our dinner," Mason said.

He'd gone through a lot of work and I was impressed by it. What woman wouldn't be? Whether we admitted it or not, most of us savored the thought of being treated like a queen on a date. I know that I did, although I wasn't prepared to admit that to Mr. Mason Beast quite yet—maybe ever.

The tour of the mansion was amazing. It was so interesting to see his family's history through all the paintings and photos that were in the house. There was even a room that was like a mini-museum, devoted to the entire history of Beast Stores. It had original sketches from fashion shows that they'd hosted, as well as exclusive lines. There were endless autographed pictures of famous designers and celebrities that were connected to the store in some way. Really incredible.

Mason pointed to a blank space on the wall. "Soon, your mother will be hanging there, I hope."

That concept touched me profoundly. Knowing that Mom and I were the beginning of our history, having a spot amongst all the icons on the walls seemed so special. I smiled, imagining how Mom would react to that. She'd be composed and grateful upfront, but the second we were alone, she'd jump up in the air and do that fun little dance she liked to do in private when she was excited. I was so proud of her.

"How long has your family owned this mansion, Mason?"

"My great-great-grandfather actually took it over when one of his designers couldn't pay back money that he owed. He'd fallen upon hard times."

"Now that is the way to get a mansion, I suppose," I said, nodding my head. Talk about being in the right place at the right time.

"He was a shrewd man and a pack-rat, which is how all this is possible," Mason said. "We have everything from the store's first opening back in 1902."

"Everything? You mean advertisements, things like that?"

"Yes, plus some of the clothes, as well. There were certain pieces that my grandparents thought were exquisite—almost like art to some—and they saved them all. It's quite the collection."

"Can I see it?" I asked. I loved vintage clothing.

We made our way to an upstairs room with a massive walk-in closet. The closet was at least 3,000 square feet, a pretty decent sized home in California for the average person.

I began to walk through the closet, almost afraid to touch all the dresses with their sequins, rich and lustrous fabrics, and stunning colors—all very well preserved considering they were not covered with anything. "Mason, you should really have these in vacuum sealed bags or something. They're too beautiful to let the elements ruin them, especially being so close to the ocean."

"All covered, Charisma," he said, putting his hand in his pocket and leaning against a dresser in the center of the room and staring at me.

"How so?"

"This closet has special lighting in it to preserve them, and when the door is shut, you can just press a button and it creates a vacuum of sorts for further protection. The motto of the family has always been that fashion is meant to be worn and touched, not just stared at."

"That's a beautiful sentiment," I said.

"I agree. So…what do you say we have a little fashion show?" he asked.

"You mean we can wear these, Mason?"

"Absolutely. Personally, I like the vintage Armani tux and that's what I'm going with first."

"I don't know how I'd decide," I said, my jaw unhinged. This was so cool!

"Allow me to pick then," he said.

Beautiful Girl: Modern Beauty and Beast (Happy Ever After Standalone Novel Series)

I watched Mason and he went right over to a 20s flapper dress that was red. He pulled it off the hanger and commented, "Perfect." Then he continued on, getting a hat, a strand of pearls, and some shoes.

"Why don't you use the changing room over there," he said. "I can't wait to see what you look like."

I walked into the changing room, which was beautiful in and of itself—very French inspired. I slid off my jeans and t-shirt and put on the clothes that Mason had picked out and assessed myself in the mirror. They were stunning. I don't know how he just knew what would look good on me, but he had obvious flare for it. *Must run in the family*, I thought.

I exited the changing room and said, "So, what do you think?"

One look at Mason and I knew. He appreciated what he saw. And I appreciated what I saw, too. He looked so handsome in that tux and the way he stood there, looking at me, I almost felt like I was transported back to some speak-easy in the 20s. It was all so wildly romantic—and fun!

From there, we kept changing into different clothes, deciding to span every decade. We were laughing and talking and playing dress-up like two kids might, but there was a very adult chemistry between the two of us.

I walked out in my 70s garb and looked at Mason, who was in his, and the two of us started laughing. "Definitely a struggle for fashion in this decade," I said.

"I agree. I can't imagine. Tight in all the wrong places," he said.

His eyes moved downward and I found myself staring at his crotch. Those pants were definitely tight on it, emphasizing its enormity. He must be very well endowed from the size of his bulge. Even though I've never done it before, I wondered how it must feel to have such a large penis enter. I was a virgin at 22 years old, but I wasn't so naïve about sex. I wanted it just like any other woman, but I wanted it at the right time and with the right guy. And I wanted it to be the most amazing sex, the most pleasurable and hot sex I could ever experience. If a man can't give me hot sex, can't be passionate with me, then I'd have to pass. Could Mason be the one who could give me everything I want in a man? Including mind-blowing can't walk the next day sex? I blushed picturing him naked, on top of me, and making me scream as he rammed into me; and almost stumbled. Embarrassed and noticing Mason's smiling eyes on me, I changed the subject.

***

"Mason, this zipper is stuck and I don't want to tug," I said, walking out into the large room and staring at him.

He walked over and I turned around. With his hands on my shoulders, I felt the heated power of his touch that almost made me jump with its intense sensuality. I could tell from the electricity between us how he wanted me.

"Allow me," he whispered hoarsely in my ear, his chest pressed against my back from behind. The fabric of his shirt tickled my skin and when his hands went to the zipper to try and loosen it, his lips began kissing my neck so tenderly. I could barely breathe. When he lightly licked the hollow of my neck, I gasped from pleasure.

"Liked that?" he whispered against my cheek, "there's a lot more where that came from, baby, and I can't wait to lick you all over from your beautiful head to your toes. And inside you." He groaned. "Especially inside you. I've been wanting to taste you from the moment I set my eyes on you and your sexy sweet body."

Oh God, he was so sexy. I felt myself start to heat up from the core of me.

I'm not sure how it happened, even, but I heard the sound of unzipping and felt the dress fall down to my ankles, sending a small breeze over me, making me shiver. There I was, exposed in my lingerie and feeling so aroused by the hot, steamy kisses that Mason was so masterfully delivering. His arms wrapped around me and he lifted me up, carrying me over toward the bed in the corner.

My mind was going wild. I wasn't sure I wanted to lose my virginity to him, despite all this, but I was so excited and turned on by the entire night up to that point. I didn't want to say no, but I wasn't prepared to say yes, either.

"Don't worry," Mason said, staring right into my eyes. It was like he could read my mind and I just trusted that he had, curious about what else he could do to keep this sensual feeling alive inside of me. I wanted to be the naughty girl and scream, "Fuck me." But I also wanted to be selfish and enjoy what he may deliver, continuing my reign as the queen I felt like I was.

"Mmm," I said as he placed me gently on the bed and leaned down and gave my inner thigh a feathery kiss.

"I'm going to savor every inch of your creamy, perfect flesh," he said. "Can I do that, Charisma?"

I nodded my head, temporarily speechless from the seductive words. And also a bit of anticipation that was shouting, "Get to it, already! You have me, now take me."

He groaned loudly and said, "Mercy me, Charisma. You are so beautiful I'm going to enjoy dining on you tonight." Then he dove between my thighs and became very passionate and more intense; unleashing what seemed to be another side of him. A beastly sex-driven wild side to him. The Mason I knew from the office was gone. Instead, here was this sexy uninhibited man who could not get enough of me. He licked me so intensely and so hard, I was grabbing the soft silky comforter beneath me. I felt like a wild animal had been unleashed, and was ravenous for sex. Was starved for the taste of me. He couldn't get enough.

"So delicious, Charisma," he groaned between licks and kisses. "This isn't enough, baby. I want to fill my mouth with you." His entire hot mouth covered my sex, and he licked me before inhaling and sucking me deeply.

I cried out, "Oh so good."

Beautiful Girl: Modern Beauty and Beast (Happy Ever After Standalone Novel Series)

The way his tongue flickered on my flesh made me feel like he was the devil in the form of a snake tempting me to go to the dark side with him. I've never experienced such mind-blowing pleasure.

"I want more of you," Mason said, looking into my eyes with hunger. "I want to make you mine."

His mouth fell again on my pussy, licking it with full abandon. My back arched unwillingly as he slid my panties completely off, turned me around so my back was facing him, and pulled me up on my knees. He began to suck on me hard, his tongue darting in and out of me, reaching my G until I was gasping. I was going to explode from the unbelievable pleasure. In and out. In and out.

"Oh God," I cried out. "Oh Mason."
"Not yet," Mason chuckled deeply. The vibrations of his chuckle deep in his throat nearly sent me over the edge. He continued with the onslaught. It was hypnotic and rhythmic. Then he'd mix it up, sliding his fingers in with his tongue and putting pressure in all the right spots. I felt my juices covering his hand and I was

coming with no control over it. "That's it, baby," Mason groaned, licking my juices and closing his eyes savoring me. "Keep going, baby. Just let go."

At that, I felt my entire body shaking harder and harder until I was screaming and convulsing. It was the hardest I've ever came, aside from my own hand and large oversize toys. Having Mason go down on me like that was no comparison. He was a sexual beast and a master at providing pleasure. He was good at everything, but when it came to sex, if that was just a sample of what he could do; he was probably one of the best fuck a woman could have.

I looked up at the ceiling and everything looked blurry, my head spinning and my heart racing as I went to a place I'd never gone before. I had no idea how much I'd love it, though, and was tantalized by just how dark I might be willing to go. I felt the desire to match Mason's intensity movement for movement, but I didn't get the chance. I could barely hear him because my heart was pounding so hard and the blood rushing through my body, but he said, "We'd better take a break and eat. The chef may be wondering where we are…although I doubt his feast could be as good as the one I just experienced."

I was let down and I was relieved. When I'd woken up that morning I'd never thought it would be a day where I lost my virginity, if you count oral sex as sex.

"Are you good with what I did?" Mason asked me tenderly, moving a strand of my hair behind my ear.

"Wow, yes," I said bluntly. Really, what would the point of denying it be? He'd sent me skyrocketing with his actions.

"Good, I just want you to know how patient I am and that you're becoming a very special woman to me, Charisma. I definitely want more of you, but for now, it turns me on just to pleasure you. In time, we'll get more playful, and try more daring things, but for now, since it's your first time…that's enough."

***

After I took a shower and ate dinner with Mason whose eyes never left my face, I was still on a pleasurable high. Nothing could sour my night, except not being able to continue what we started.

"Bad news," Mason said, looking at me. His face didn't seem to be worked up about anything in particular, though.

"Oh no, everything okay?" I asked.

"We just took too long out on the island. There's a small storm front setting in and we can't get clearance to head back to the mainland. So...we're stuck here tonight."

"How convenient," I said with a smirk.

"Indeed," he replied, staring at me with ravenous eyes. Those eyes may very well be the death of me.

Well, it didn't rain at all that night, because I could barely sleep. There I was in this amazing bed in my own guest room—comfortable and luxurious—and all I had on my mind was what Mason had done to me. That darker side of him was really hot and sexy, and definitely unexpected. It was a huge draw, and I was seriously curious to experience more of this beastly side of him.

When I went down to the kitchen area the next morning, Mason was sitting at the breakfast counter, drinking a cup of coffee, and reading the Wall Street Journal.

"Good morning," he said, jumping up and coming over to give me a soft kiss on the cheek. "Hopefully you slept well."

"Slept great," I said. Yes, I lied. I secretly wanted him to break into my room and do what he will with me last night.

"Good, if it works for you, I figured that we could take a little tour of the island today, have some fun."

"I'd love that," I said. I had only been to Catalina Island once before, and I was pretty young. Somehow, I thought a private tour with a hot billionaire might be a little different. Mason proved me right. Everything was enchanted and perfect, from the golf carts along the coastal path to the glass bottom boat that was chartered just for the two of us. It seemed like he wanted me to himself, and I didn't mind that he did. Before I knew it, the sun was setting again.

"So, are you up for spending one more night on the island?" Mason asked. "Compared to me making some excuse as to why you should."

"Was last night an excuse?" I asked. I hadn't thought it was at all, until that moment.

"No, that was legit, but right now, I could take you back if you wanted. Of course what I really want is for you to stay. We could have a picnic on the catwalk and look at the stars. They're out in full force tonight.

That is so romantic, I thought. *This thing, whatever it is, is crazy exciting.*

"I think I can do one more night. I'd better call my mom, though, and let her know what's going on," I said.

"I'll leave you to it," he said. "You call and I'll get the picnic prepared."

"Not the staff?" I asked.

"No, they can't help me put together what I want for this," he said with a coy smile. His double talk was making me twice as aroused as I'd ever been in my life.

I pulled out my phone and called home.
"Hello?" a male voice said. It was strange hearing Callum answer, because I just wasn't used to that completely despite it all.

"Callum, hi, I just wanted to let you know that I won't be home until tomorrow," I said.

"Where are you at?" he asked in a curt tone.

This would be a bit strange. "At your family's home on Catalina Island."

"With Mason?" he asked.

"Well, yes," I said.

"Okay then, I'll let your mother know," he said. Then he hung up, leaving me with a strange feeling about his icy tone. It made me instantly feel nervous, but I didn't really understand why.

Chapter 13

Charisma

"Good morning," Mason said, staring over me and shaking my shoulder gently. "Breakfast is served, Madam."

"What?" I asked, rubbing my eyes and hoping that I didn't look like a wild mess that morning. I'd slept soundly after barely sleeping the night before.

"I made us breakfast and it'll be served on the balcony off my bedroom," he said, smiling at me.

"If your intent on our casual date was to spoil me, you've done a wonderful job, Mason."

"That's great to hear. You're worth spoiling," he said. He offered his hand and I looked down to make sure that no parts of me were exposed. Rather silly, I suppose, since he'd ravaged me like crazy just two nights ago. I couldn't stop thinking about it, and wanting more. And admittedly, I was a bit thrown off that he hadn't tried it again. True to his word, he was being a gentleman and taking it slow. Maybe he was waiting for me to make the next move.

We walked out onto his balcony and sat down in the two comfortable chairs overlooking the ocean. In the center of the table was a bowl of fruit, croissants, and two heated chafing dishes. "I made eggs and sausage. Hopefully that works," he said.

"It does," I said, sitting down. "It smells so good, thanks for putting this together, Mason."

"My pleasure. Do you want some orange juice?" he asked.

"That would be great." I watched him get up and oh my gosh—he started to fresh squeeze the orange juice.

I couldn't believe it. This weekend definitely made up the ultimate date.

After he handed me my juice, Mason reached over and took my hand. "I have to tell you something kind of sudden, Charisma."

"Sure, what is it?"

Mason breathed in deeply and then exhaled. The breeze from the ocean was gently blowing his hair, too, making him look even more handsome. "Ever since my father died, knowing that he never got to become a grandfather—something he wanted badly—I've really been thinking about life and what's important. Life is too short to waste and to not go after what you want. I'm lucky, because I know what I want and I've gotten it up until this point. There's only one missing piece."

"What's that?" I asked, my voice barely above a whisper.

"A woman to share it with. And Charisma, I think that may be you. I know I have feelings for you and they're growing deeper with each minute we spend together. I know it's sudden and I don't want to scare you, but please know that I am not like my brother and that if I were to offer myself to you, it would be because of my heart. I'd treat you like you were my entire world. I want you to know that I am not my brother and until the day I die, I'll be ashamed of the way he treated you and your mother."

Mason's words were so impassioned by his emotions and I saw how genuine they were, but at that moment I realized something crazy; something that hadn't crossed my mind. He had no idea where Callum was.

"So, how is Callum doing with his recovery?" I asked. Maybe a bit of a loaded question, but I had to gauge Mason.

Mason's face darkened at my question and he leaned back and looked me in the eyes as he expressed himself. "Frankly Charisma, I don't know. And after what he's done, I don't care, either. He made his bed and now he's lying in it, and if he gets a taste of how other people who were less fortunate than him treat him now, then that's good. He needs to grow up and stop being an embarrassment to this family."

The past weeks had been crazy and in a way, Callum had become a part of my family. He took on a role within it and never complained—helping with meals, cleaning, watching TV with us, and even doing some of the heavy lifting that we'd always had to get help to do. "He's come a long way since that night," I said softly.

"What? How do you know that?" Mason was now leaning in and looking at me with scrutiny in his eyes that hadn't been there just a second before.

I smiled weakly and said, "Well, I was shocked at first, but he's staying with us…"

Mason cut me off and slapped his fist down on the table, making it rattle a bit. "What? You mean at your house with you and your mom?" He was shaking his head back and forth.

"Yeah, surprisingly," I said, feeling a bit awkward now. "My mom opened the door for him to stay in our guest room. He had nowhere else to go and he was visiting my mom to apologize, but Mom put him to work for us and gave him a place to stay."

Mason looked angry and then jealous. It was noticeable. His hand clenched into a fist, and his jaws tighten. "And you never thought to tell me this? I don't even see how you could forgive him. He's an ass. Much less let him into your home and your work environment. He's toxic."

"Mason..." I began, but clamped my lips together. He wasn't done.

"Do you see him every day? At work? What about at home?"

I nodded yes. "I know, it's hard to believe, but Mom believes in paying it forward, and in karma. She is also incredibly grateful for every single blessing she's ever received so she could never have any hate for anyone…at least not for long."

"I'll say," Mason said. "Your mother is truly one of a kind just like you are."

Mason got up and walked around the table and gave me a kiss on the lips, hard and urgent. It reminded me of an animal claiming its territory. "He hasn't seen you naked, has he?" he asked, a hiss in his voice.

"No, and knock it off, Mason. We live in the same house so he sees me at my worst, sweats, no make-up on, and it's casual. It is not a big deal."

"Does he leave you alone?" he asked, now on a rant again.

"I'm not sure what you mean. We have a routine. I drive him to work since he lost his license, we talk every day. This weekend is the first time I haven't seen him for a day since he moved in."

"I see," Mason said, clenching his jaw. "That weasel. He knew I was interested in you."

"He's never mentioned anything like that. Honestly Mason, I think he's just grateful to be able to have a place to stay and a job."

"Modeling make-up to hide his scars," Mason spat.

"Ouch. That's pretty cold," I said, not liking that tone.

"Charisma, don't you see that Callum hates you and your mother enough that he's willing to take his joke this far. He'll get the last laugh on you, because he's a bastard. I don't trust him with you, or your mother. I guarantee you that he's going to try to get close to you and steal your virginity and brag it up to his frat friends.

It's one of his favorite conquests. If I was your mother,
I'd kick him out right away."

"But this is your own brother you're talking
about," I justified. "I don't understand. Why would
anyone be that cruel and mean?"

"There are mean people out there, people who
would lie to you, befriend you even, and when you trust
them the most, they will stab you in the back. I've seen it
a lot with Father's friends and colleagues. I know Callum
Beast, although he's my brother, would be like that to get
ahead, or even to win. He'll play dirty, Charisma. He'll
infiltrate into your company and your home, steal your
company's secrets and seduce you. Then break your
heart. He'll hurt you again. Don't trust him."

"I'll be careful around him, then," I said, still
feeling like Mason was overreacting a bit. It had to be
jealousy, because the way he spoke was not the way
people really acted, was it? "But remember, it isn't my
decision about him staying at the house or working at the
company. It's my mother's."

"Just be prepared to act when his true colors show, and don't say that I didn't warn you, Charisma."

After that conversation, I lost some enthusiasm for my Catalina adventure, and Mason did, too. We ended up going home early and Mason dropped me off. Before I got out of the car, he gave me a long and deep kiss. It was different than the others had been, because it was a "gotcha kiss." You know, one that was for the purpose of getting even with his brother, rather than pleasing me. I was disappointed, but I did understand.

"Mason, I did have an incredible weekend, thank you," I said. "And, I'll keep in mind what you told me, too."

"Good," he said, reverting back to the man who could look at me with a killer sexy expression.

I walked into the house just to find that no one was home. But on the kitchen table there was a note.

Charisma,
Your mother and I went out for a combination of
work and fun adventure. We didn't realize that
you'd be gone for the entire weekend.
Callum

I felt a lump in my throat and wasn't sure what to
think of the note. It worried me. What if Callum wasn't
to be trusted? What if he really wanted to get close to us
just to hurt us, especially my mother? Whatever his
intentions were, I wanted to find out what they were as
quickly as possible. I'd do anything I had to in order to
protect my mother.

Chapter 14

Charisma

My heart was racing and I felt so unsettled. I'd sold myself on the fact that Callum was changing, but Mason's words made me second guess myself, leaving me agonizing over Mom's safety. Where did they go?

I called Mom, relieved that she answered right away. She sounded really, happy. "Are you okay?" I asked cautiously.

"Fantastic," she said and then she laughed and I heard her say, "Oh Callum" with her mouth away from the phone.

"Where are you at?" I asked, trying to sound relaxed, but feeling like my stomach was dropping out like I was going downhill fast on a thrill ride.

"We're over at the Moon Festival Celebration,"
Mom said.

As soon as she said that, I remembered. We were
doing the contestant's make-up as a fun way to launch the
Heavenly Beauty line. How could I have forgotten?
"Mom, I'm sorry. It completely slipped my mind. Do I
still have time to get down there?"

"Don't worry, honey. You were having fun. It's
okay. If it works out, it would be great if you could come
down here. I tried to call Stryker to see if he could come
and do photos, but he's out of town."

"I'll be down there as quickly as I can and send
you a text when I enter the festival grounds," I said.

We hung up and I quickly changed, finding a t-
shirt and jeans to put on, along with some fun sandals.
The Moon Festival was a fun event, filled with interesting
people, beautiful decorations, and yummy food. I was
shocked that I'd forgotten. Mason had me in such a

tailspin that I'd just lost my senses, I guess. I was grateful to Callum for going with her to it.

With my camera in hand, I charged out of the house and into the garage and then drove off, heading toward LA. The traffic wasn't too heavy because it was the weekend—thank goodness and I made relatively good time. Where I lost that time was finding a place to park downtown. There was a lot of action—sporting events, festivals, and even a parade for something or another, I wasn't sure what. By the time I found a parking space, I had to walk about a half mile just to enter the festival grounds.

Pulling my phone back out I called Mom, but Callum answered her phone. "Hey, she's talking with the contestants, but told me to wait for your call," he said to me.

"Oh, where are you guys at?" I asked. This was so strange. I just wanted to see Mom and make sure—with my own eyes—that she was okay.

"We're over by the stage. I'm under the large paper mâché cherry blossom tree. You can't miss it," Callum said.

"See you in a few," I said. I hung up and began to navigate my way through the crowd, taking in the festivities and scents of the event. It really was quite magical and special, a beautiful tribute to the Asian culture and how nicely it could be infused with the western world.

I made my way toward the tall paper mâché cherry tree and Callum was right about it being hard to miss. That tree was incredible; must have taken an entire year to make. Intricate details that made it seem quite real from a distance and the illusion didn't change the closer I got. My mother' shiny black hair with a slight streak of gray finally came into view. She was polished, as always, wearing a beautiful silk dress that fit the occasion perfectly. And next to her was Callum, although his back was to me. I immediately noticed his broad shoulders, despite them being covered by a plaid shirt and jeans that showed just how muscular his legs were. When he turned around, I almost gasped. He really was good looking and I saw his muscular chest because his shirt was unbuttoned just enough to tease me with it.

From where I was at that moment, you'd never have known that the beautiful Callum Beast had ever been in an accident. Between the skin treatments he'd been receiving, the medical attention, and his work-outs, he looked just like that underwear model. It was only when I got up close that I could see those scars. I'd been around him so much that I'd forgotten how good looking he was, exactly. Well, I was reminded at that moment and it was distracting. What were these Beast brothers trying to do to me?

"Charisma, dear," Mom said, smiling at me and waving me over.

"Hi, looks like you guys are having fun," I said, smiling at the two of them. Mom looked like she was glowing, at ease and completely relaxed. That was good! It meant that Callum hadn't been saying anything that wasn't kind. If he had, I know I would have been able to read it on my mother's face.

"This is amazing," Callum said, almost in forced eagerness, but when I looked at him, his eyes were smiling. Beautiful smiling eyes. "Helen has been so kind as to teach me all sorts of things. I've even tried a few things."

"Yeah, like what?" I asked, tilting my head. My hair fell over my shoulder and I watched him curiously.

"I tried some paper mâché, an authentic bowl of Chinese noodles. Did you know that American Chinese is different from native Chinese?" His eyes were so expressive.

I laughed. "Yes, I knew that, Callum."

"Of course," he replied, playfully palming his forehead. "Really, though, I can't believe that I've never been to this before."

"Your frat friends don't do festivals?" I asked in lighthearted sarcasm.

"Definitely not, but I'm not so sure if they're my friends, Charisma."

Mom came over to me and said, "I've been asked to judge, Charisma, so, if you don't mind, could you make sure Callum has a fun time—and take some pictures." She had a sly smile on her face.

"No problem," I said, looking at her curiously. She was up to something, but why? And what?

Then she walked away, leaving me with a few quick thoughts. First, I was absolutely delighted to see how happy she was and that Callum was being so respectful with her. He'd been since he lived with us, of course, but I still had a hard time assuming that's how he'd remain. I guess I was waiting for him to expose his real self, if it was different, or any ulterior motives he may have.

"Do you want to stand backstage? I'll be running around taking pictures." I looked at Callum and his arms were folded casually, making him seem so relaxed and approachable. If I didn't know better, I would have thought it was his alter ego—definitely not the Callum I first met.

"I'd rather be a part of the crowd," he said. "I must say, Helen is so talented at putting make-up on. Those shades are exquisite."

My jaw wanted to drop, but it didn't. "You are getting into make-up, aren't you?"

"Well, you always wear it for shoots, I guess, but the last few weeks of being around the cosmetics company and spending time with you and your mother…well, let's just say I have a new appreciation for it."

"That's nice to say," I said.

"I meant it, Charisma." That was all he said and then he turned back toward the stage, clapping and watching the pageant enthusiastically. I was impressed, thinking that he definitely had more of a capacity to kick back and relax and enjoy the various adventures that life had to offer than Mason did. From the same blood, but so different.

An hour later the pageant was done and Mom came back over by us. "So, what did you two think? The winner was quite lovely, yes?"

"Very striking. She photographed well," I said.

"Good, because while I didn't announce it, my thoughts were that she could be our signature face for the Heavenly Beauty line. What do you think, Charisma?"

"That's a great idea," I said, always in awe of my mom's insight into things and how to make the most out of every situation—professionally and personally.

"And what do you think, Callum?" she asked.

"You want my opinion?" he commented, looking genuinely humbled.

Mom nodded her head subtly and said, "Of course, you know the camera better than anyone here."

"I think she'd be fantastic. Her right side is a bit better than her left, but hey, we all have a better side, right?" Then he laughed. He was joking at himself, which made me laugh along with him.

"Very well said, Callum," Mom said. "Now, if you two don't mind, I think that I'll head home and leave you two to it. I'm quite tired and have to go over the quarterly statements for the accountant later."

"Let me walk you to your car," Callum offered. Then he turned to me. "I'll meet you back here in about fifteen minutes, okay?"

"Sure," I said.

I hugged Mom and then watched as Callum and her walked off, his hand gently on her elbow, guiding her through the busy crowd. My mind was in a haze as I tried to process it all. Every warning Mason had given me seemed blown up and overstated. I really felt that Callum had changed for the better, and that was wonderful to see. My mother was so magical and insightful about human nature, forcing people to bring out the best in themselves—despite themselves. If she believed Callum had changed, than I should too, shouldn't I?

Chapter 15

Charisma

We had so much fun at the festival and time
started to fly by. I was really touched when I watched
Callum start playing some games with a sweet little girl.
He was doing all sorts of silly things, like acting like a
monkey, and it made her giggle so hard. She just stared at
him like he was the most amazing person she'd ever seen,
and I didn't blame her.

"He's Prince Pretty!" the little girl exclaimed to
her mother who was smiling in delight. I was kind of
feeling that way, too. The highlight was when she
managed to beat him at the game, which got her so
excited that she was jumping up and down, clapping, and
even teasing him about it a little bit. He played his role
well, and I was moved by his commitment to it.

"Did you get some good pictures?" Callum asked me, walking over after his crushing defeat.

"I did. Maybe we can walk around so I can get a few more before it gets too dark out."

"That'll be great. Can I see what you got?" he asked.

I turned on the camera and we started to look at the small screen on the back of it and I was a bit embarrassed to realize that almost every picture I'd taken was one with Callum in it. That wasn't my intention, but it definitely was what happened.

"Definitely time to photograph something else," he said. I looked at him and saw a bit of sadness on his face.

"What's wrong?" I asked.

"Just not a fan of seeing my picture, I guess," he
said honestly.

"You don't have anything to be self-conscious
about," I said. He only smiled at me and then started to
walk. I never would have thought I'd see such a
vulnerable side to him and it made me have this crazy
desire to make everything better—like he was some
wounded animal I'd found.

"Hey, look over there, it looks like kites. Let's go
check it out." I knew that he'd changed the topic, and I
felt bad about it, but I was eager to go and spend some
time with him. Plus, the kites looked amazing—definitely
the type of thing a photo enthusiast like me would
appreciate.

***

"What's your favorite, Callum?" I asked, looking
into the sky as it grew a bit darker and the kites, all
illuminated in one way or another, floated about the sky
like they were pure magic.

"The one that looks like a dragon—love the glowing eyes," he said, smiling and pointing at it like he was a small child. He seemed so innocent at that moment, which was so contrary to what I knew he truly was... Maybe I'd been wrong. "How about you, Charisma? Which one do you like?"

"That one," I said, pointing to the lantern that was softly illuminated and floating in the sky, reminding me of a wayward ghost that didn't know where to go. It was definitely me—or my emotional thoughts, I should say— at that moment.

"Interesting choice. Subtle and understated, quite perfect for you actually," Callum said.

I looked at him and saw him leaning in toward me. Oh no! He was going to kiss me. I took a step back, suddenly feeling crazy, but I landed in a small dip in the ground and my ankle twisted, making me crumble down and take a fall backwards, where I realized how close I was to the small manmade lake. Splash! I landed in it, my entire body getting drenched. Holding out my arm, with the camera in my hand, I had saved the camera though.

"Charisma!" Callum called out in shock, but his strong muscular arm was already extended out, ready to save me.

I looked at him and then around me. People were watching me, but they were also watching him. He really was a good looking man, too good looking for my own good, and his.

Attempting to stand up and regain my dignity, I was met with a piercing pain and plummeted back down on my butt. I grimaced from the shot of intense and searing pain that came from my ankle.

"Charisma, what's wrong?" Callum asked, rushing into the water next to me.

"My ankle, I think I twisted it," I said, feeling very uncomfortable with all the eyes that were on me. Some gasped sympathetically and some laughed. It was quite the sight, but my ankle hurt.

"Let me help you," Callum said. He leaned down and lifted me up, my body pressed into his muscular chest and carried me out of the water. I looked down at my ankle and saw that it was beginning to swell.

Once he had me out of the water I smiled, pretty embarrassed, and said, "Thanks for fishing me out and not letting go."

"I'd never let you go," he said. His voice was so touching and soft, making me feel like a ghost had just blown a sexy, seductive breath on my neck.

"I'm wet," I said, then blushed, realizing the innuendo. Callum's eyes showed that he had liked the idea so I quickly added. "I guess we should take that as a hint that it's time to go. You can set me down."

"No, you shouldn't walk on that ankle. I'll carry you." His words were tender, yet authoritative. I succumbed to the notion of being the damsel in distress for just a bit. The throbbing sensations I was having were a good reminder that it wasn't the time to be stubborn about walking.

With a graceful gait, Callum carried me to my car and then gently set me down in the back seat of it, where I could elevate my leg to hopefully reduce the swelling. "I should stop at a convenience store for some ice," he offered.

"No, we can wait until we get home," I said, smiling at him. "Thanks for taking such good care of me."

"It's my pleasure," he said in a silky tone. "Here, let's make a temporary bandage for that to keep the swelling down."

I watched him and before I could say anything, he was taking off his shirt and leaning over to gently wrap it around my ankle. His shirtless bare body hovered over mine as he tried to be gentle and the heat from it barely touching me aroused me quickly, consuming me like a sudden dizzy spell throws you off kilter. My pulse quickened and I found that I really was growing wetter from my thoughts and the unavoidable closeness between us. What was this chemistry? I shook slightly.

"Are you cold?" he asked.

I nodded, not wanting to admit that I was.

Without another word, Callum's lips crashed against mine and he groaned. "Oh Charisma," he whispered like he was out of breath. "Don't hate me for kissing you, but I can't help what I feel for you. I can't hold back any longer. I love you. So much."

Did I hear him correctly? What was going on. We were so close and I didn't know what to say so I started with, "Callum, I don't hate you. I thought I would always hate you, but I can't."

He looked at me and tenderness filled his intense green eyes. "Really? You don't know how much that means to me...I'm so grateful and relieved. I know that you could never love me, because of how I acted, but I do want to change. You inspire me. I want to be a better person for you, Charisma. I'd do anything for you, anything to make things right between us and for you to see me as a man who'd go to the ends of this earth to prove himself worthy of you."

"Callum," I said, my eyes wide open as I stared at the poetic, yet tormented words he spoke to me. He was unapologetic and passionate and I couldn't help but respond to it.

He kept talking. "When you went off on your date with Mason, it nearly killed me, Charisma. I was so jealous. I shouldn't be, but I was, and…I know you probably feel something for Mason…especially over me, but I'm struggling. I love you so much. I think about you all the time. I dream of you. You are the one person who has kept this hell I'm in bearable. I lost my family. I lost my inheritance. I can't lose you, too."

Now he trembled. "I don't understand," I said softly.

"I just want you too much to be quiet and step aside. I have to fight for you," Callum replied. Again, his directness and apparent honesty were so sincere, melting my heart and making me see him in such a different way than I had to that point. But it was too much.

"Callum, I don't want you to fight for me."

"What? Am I not even a good enough rival for Mason for you?"

I felt his body stiffen and in the small, confined space he tried to retract. "No, let me explain," I said. "I'm not a piece of meat or a prize for two men to fight over. I don't even know how I feel. All this is new to me, and…"

I watched those amazing green eyes change colors, going from darkness to a brighter shade that was obvious even in the fading light of day. "So there is still a chance to win you!" His enthusiasm was unbridled and I saw a competitive side of him that showed that he didn't hesitate to pursue what he wanted. And he wanted me. Crazy. "As long as there's a chance to win you I'm going to give it all I've got, Charisma. Maybe I'll be the winner and you'll fall in love with me."

"I really don't know if there's a chance or not," I said honestly, feeling a bit trapped now. "This is all new to me and even when Mason came down..." I clamped my lips, wanting to kick myself for letting that slip.

"What?" Callum's eyes burned with fury. "He what?"

I blushed, so embarrassed that I had done that. "Please forget I said that."

"No," Callum said. "He tried to seduce you, and I...I..." He found his way out of the car, leaving me sitting in the backseat and feeling like a complete idiot.

"Callum," I began, but he turned his back to me.

I heard him say, "Just give me a second...fresh air..." and something else. Then he turned around and put his arm on the roof of the car and leaned in to look at me closer. "Did he go further than that?"

This felt so private to share, especially talking to Callum about his brother, but he wanted to know so I decided to be forthright. "No, he was a perfect gentleman, and I hate to admit it, but I wanted more," I said. "I'd never experienced that kind of pleasure before and it was exciting. I loved feeling that way and...well, I hope I can again. Do you know what I mean?"

"Enlighten me," he said, tension showing on his face.

"That place where you're reacting to what your body is feeling and not over thinking everything. I'd never felt so free, and well, I liked that."

Callum leaned back into the car and took my hands in his. I felt their warmth, their tenderness. "I didn't know you wanted to experience that. I don't want to sound perverted or cross, but please, Charisma, ask me anything you'd like. About any of it. I've had my share of it, and…"

"I want to feel it again, Callum." My statement had determination and I meant it, that physical feeling was seared in me and I wanted it again.

Callum gulped and cautiously said, "Even if it's not with Mason?"

"I don't know," I confessed. "If Mason is the only one who could make me feel this way…"

"No, he isn't," Callum said quickly and adamantly, cutting me off. "He's not the best, he's too selfish, and some of us guys…me…have a lot more experience in this area than he does and I want to so desperately to bring you pleasure. I dreamed about it so often, I wake up soaked…"

"Show me," I interjected.

"Really?" Callum was shocked and I liked having that power over him, I'll admit. He didn't hesitate, though, and crawled back out of the car and looked at me. "I know I'm not supposed to drive, but you can't with your ankle. I know a good place to take you, we can get some ice for your ankle and I can take care of you."

"I'd like that," I said, very aware of how my stomach was doing flips in anticipation. I really wasn't so easy, but if what I was feeling towards Mason just because of how he pleasured me, then I wasn't sure if it was that I wanted more of or him? At the same time, Callum made me feel that same heated feeling inside, and I didn't know if it was because I was drawn to him as a person or sexually too. Mason was becoming more and more serious, and I wasn't sure if I wanted that commitment too, at least not yet.

That hot feeling of seeing Callum, especially without his shirt on, and that searing hungry look in his eyes for me did not subside even when a half hour later, Callum was carrying me into the Otani Hotel, where he'd gotten us a room. It was embarrassing seeing the faces of everyone watch us walk by, me in Callum's arms, while the women in the hotel lobby and front desk stared at Callum with lustful eyes.

I felt like a harlot, but at the same time, bold and daring. I had been obedient and careful with myself my entire life until meeting Mason and Callum. If I wanted to give my heart to any man, either of them, I wanted to see if any of them could satisfy my wild desires as well.

Chapter 16

Callum

Our bodies pressed together, my arms easily held the delicate and delicious Charisma. I couldn't wait to get her into that hotel room and take care of her every need, showing her through my actions how much I meant what I said. It scared the hell out of me, but I loved her. Yet, it also invigorated me, giving me a purpose and something to strive toward that I'd never had before. She made me feel so damn alive that it scared me. I wanted to love her. I wanted to make love to her. I also wanted to see how I could be the gentle lover who can fulfill her every desires. There was a spark in Charisma and a fire that I sensed from the beginning. It was so darn sexy and irresistible. Even Mason had fallen for her.

With the key in her hand, Charisma slid it into the door and pressed down on the handle. I kicked it open and

let it slam shut behind us, carrying her right over to the
bed and gently placing her down.

"I'll get some ice," I said.

"No," she said, looking at me with desperate eyes
filled with desire. "It can wait."

"You're sure?" I asked. No, I wasn't talking about
the ice, but about the invitation to send Charisma
skyrocketing to the moon. I didn't want to be the guy she
regretted, only to love her immensely and intensely—and
take it as far as she'd let me.

Her hands came up to my shoulders, which were
still bare from not having a t-shirt on, and she pulled me
down. I submitted to her demand, my body next to hers.
My mouth met with hers and I whispered into her mouth,
"You're so beautiful you drive me crazy." And then our
lips collided, drawn to each other like they were
magnetic, our tongues thrusting into each other's mouth
with reckless abandon and urgency. And we kept kissing
until we were forced to pull apart for air.

I looked into her eyes, hoping there would be no hesitation, and there wasn't. She wanted what I wanted and it was confirmed when she looked at me and said, "Take it all off, Callum. I want to see all of you."

Man, I've never wanted a woman as much as I wanted Charisma then.

Her order was so hot, sexy, and direct; I obeyed, not saying a word. As I peeled the remainder of my clothes off I watched her as she wriggled out of hers, showing the most creamy and perfect flesh I'd ever seen. Like her face, her body was perfection. Her breasts were larger than average for someone so slim as her, and her hips flowed in a sensual curve down her lusciously round bottom. She had the body I dreamed about every night. When I saw how excited she was for me as I was for her, I wanted to whimper. Her dark nipples were erect and hard…lovely and pert. I could lick and suck on them all night. I couldn't wait to show her how much I wanted to please her—to make her gasp for air and scream for more.

She laid down on the bed, completely naked with her legs apart. Her fingers went to finger herself while I looked on hungrily. "Am I what you pictured, Callum?"

"You are my dream personified," I said deeply.

"What do you dream of doing to me, Callum?" she said licking her fingers.

I about lost it when I saw her clean each slender finger of hers with that hot tongue of hers.

"Tell me what you dream about doing to me," she said. "And do it."

"Have mercy," I groaned finally letting my control go and stumbling to Charisma on the bed.

"I dreamed about touching your smooth silky skin, Charisma..."

My hands had never felt so alive as they did when they were gliding across Charisma's flesh. I could feel her nerves jumping, alert and excited, as I moved to her breast and circled her nipple with my thumb. She threw back her head and closed her eyes, as I squeezed her nipples and bent down to taste one with my mouth.

My tongue darted out and I was licking her until she was moaning. After giving one breast so much attention, I moved to the next, sucking on it and then lightly biting it until she moaned again.

"I dream about feasting on you and..." I kissed her stomach and made my way between her legs to the honey pot I wanted to lick and eat. I sank in and licked, sucked, and ate ravenously until she was grabbing my hair with one hand and saying, "More, Callum, more!"

"You touching me here," I moved up to her and kneel in front of her so she can grasp my hard dick in her hand. "Pumping me with your hand..."

I moved her hand back and forth on my dick so she could get in the rhythm. From the way she touched me I could see that she may be a virgin, but that didn't mean she wasn't ambitious and eager when it came to claiming what she wanted. How the hell did I get so lucky

that it would be me in this spot? *Mason didn't deserve
her*, I thought. Then I quickly put him out of my mind, as
this was my moment to connect with this exquisite
creature and take her body to the moon and back.

"I dream of you taking me in your mouth and
sucking on me hard, harder than you've ever suck on a
popsicle," I groaned as she switched from pumping my
dick to licking it with her hot tongue. "Oh Charisma, you
are so good at this. A natural sex goddess."

She kissed my dick before she opened her sweet
mouth to pulled me in and began sucking hard on it.

"Oh God, woman," I cried out, trying to keep
from shaking. I almost came when I saw her wrap her
beautiful mouth around me.

Then her hands started to veer my body toward
her, my hard-on so big and thick from my excitement.
"Take me," she said. It was barely audible, yet I heard it
so clearly and felt it through her body language.

"You're sure? You really want to?" I asked. I wanted to, but I couldn't be the beast she'd thought I was—I had to show her that what she needed was most important to me.

"Callum, damn it, take me. I've waited so long for this…to find the right one, and I want it to be you." Again, simple and direct. A woman who knew what she wanted was so sexy.

"Are you sure?" I asked again.

She licked me and looked up at me. "I'm sure, Callum. Stop hesitating and give me what I want."

Fuck she was so sexy. She was a tigress in bed…wild and full of passion. But at work, she was a porcelain beauty.

I was overwhelmed with emotions as I touched Charisma, my touch turning more intimate. The woman I'd fell in love with in such a short amount of time had just offered me her greatest gift—her virginity.

"I dream of fucking you, making love to you, and making you full and satisfy…" My hand slid down her belly and my fingers entered into her wet and eager pussy. I could feel her muscles pulsating in eager anticipation turning me so hard that it almost ached. Such intensity and desire to be with someone had never happened to me before, and knowing that she wanted me fulfilled me completely.

"I'm ready, take me," she said, her hips jutting upward.

I stared right into her magnificent eyes and went on top of her, watching her every reaction and emotion as I slowly slid myself into her, feeling the warmth and tightness of her beautiful gift to me. My movements were slow in case they hurt, but she looked at me with anticipation and then relief, arching her back and closing her eyes as I thrust into her, unable to remain slow. It was urgent and I moved faster and faster, unable to slow down or stop what I'd started. I was out of control in the most amazing way and there was nothing to ruin that. My body was dictating what I'd do simply by the way her body responded. I wanted to see her have her first orgasm ever from a cock and didn't want to miss a single detail of it.

"I love you," I said, plunging into her over and over again gently and then faster.

I closed my eyes briefly because the pleasure was so great but when I opened them, I saw it, the overjoyed, mad crazy look in her eyes and the way her body was moving toward mine like it couldn't get enough. She gasped and her muscles tightened, releasing the juices of her pleasure, as she shook and cried out in pleasure.

Seeing her in such ecstasy in the peak of her orgasm, I came too, completely in sync with her, still pumping in and out of her to prolong the pleasure. We were one, together as one, in pleasure and pain. But mostly pleasure. It was a good sign, a sign that what we'd done was right and good...and meant to be. She was mine, and I was hers.

I rolled off of her and leaned over, gently kissing her breasts and enjoying her lumbered breath and hearing the pounding of her heart. She tasted so good and she was slightly sweaty, which turned me on even more. I bent and kissed her lips before lying down next to her, my fingers looking for her fingers to hold. I wanted to hold onto her, to keep touching her. She was my woman. My love of my life.

There was nothing that Charisma could do that would make me love her less. I knew it was too soon, but I wanted to tell her that I wanted her with me for the rest of my life…that I love her like I've never loved anyone before… but she completely surprised me before I could get any of my words out by saying, "Guess that just about takes the fun out of showing off your conquest of the virgin to your friends."

What did she mean by that? She wasn't a conquest, she was someone I loved, someone I was willing to do anything for, and on her terms. "What?" I asked.

She smiled and repeated it, adding, "Think about it for a second."

I did and then I finally understood. Charisma had initiated our soiree, knowing that I'd never presume that I could have her precious gift. Well, I'd gladly surrender bragging rights about her virginity, especially if I could replace them with bragging rights about her being the love of my life—my one and only, my destiny.

"Charisma," I said gently, "I don't know what you're talking about, but what we did just now, it was the most precious thing to me. I love you. I want to make love to you. And I'm sincere about being with you more than anything."

Chapter 17

Callum

Today wasn't Charisma's day to be at Beast Companies, which made it the perfect day for me to go and pay a little visit to Mason. I made up a doctor's appointment for an excuse so she wouldn't question why I wasn't by her side at the office. There were a few things that we were going to clear up and I didn't need to have anything ugly unfold in front of Charisma. I could tell he was behind the untrusting thoughts that Charisma had about me and upon further reflection, it was likely something he said that made her mention that entire conquest thing about her virginity. He could be a ruthless piece of shit sometimes, no doubt about it.

"Mr. Beast," Mason's secretary Vivian said, clearly shocked. "Can I help you?"

Kailin Gow

"I'm here to see my brother," I said walking past her and toward Mason's office.

"He's on a..." She didn't finish because my hand was already on the door to his office and I opened it up and walked in. He was on a call and my abrupt entrance startled him.

"Jim, I'll call you back in a few," Mason said. Then he hung up and leaned back in his black leather chair, looking at me analytically, the tips of his fingers now pressed together. "Callum, this is quite the surprise. Quite unnecessary, a call would have been sufficient."

"What I have to say to you needs to be said face to face, man to man," I said.

"Now that's rich," Mason said, giving a snide chuckle.

"How could you do it? That's what I want to know," I said.

"Do what?" he asked, looking genuinely perplexed.

"Put such deceitful thoughts about the type of man I was into Charisma's mind," I said. I could feel my body shaking and I had to remember to keep my anger in check.

"Me? I'd hardly need to do that. She saw the type of man you are, Callum, and what an embarrassment you are to this family with the way you behave."

"You said that she'd better watch out or I'd seduce her," I said, seething now. My fingers hurt from clenching my fists and trying to control my urge to lunge right over that desk and smack Mason across the jaw.

"Isn't that true, though? You'd love to have a conquest like a virgin, especially with a woman as beautiful as Charisma. She deserves better," Mason said.

She did deserve the best, but my brother was wrong. "There is no way in hell that I'd ever manipulate her that way, Mason."

Kailin Gow

"I can see it now, the way you and your frat brothers would laugh about it, thinking it was something," Mason said.

"They're your frat brothers, too, Mason."

"We're not tight the way you are so don't bother trying to pull that shit, Callum. It isn't going to work with me."

"Well, this accident has changed a lot. I don't hang out with any of those guys anymore. I'm a new and better man. I've changed. I care deeply about Charisma."

"You may be able to convince others of that, but not me. I know you too well, and I've known you too long," Mason said snidely. "The only person you care about is yourself."

"You don't know me at all, brother. You may want to be the big shot around here, but let me remind you

that Father still wanted me to run this company, not you,
and I would be right now if it wasn't for the accident."

"Oh, the accident that killed him?" Mason asked.
I saw the snicker in his eyes and he knew his words would
sting me. He was being a cold son-of-a-bitch, for certain.

"I will be running this company sooner than you
know," I said. I would do whatever it took to show that I
was a good man for Charisma—as smart in the business
world as committed to her pleasure in bed.

"Running it into the ground, maybe. Look,
Callum, this has been nice, but now I've got to get back
to the real world and run a business. So, if you'll excuse
me." He got up to walk over to his credenza.

Unable to stop myself, I lunged toward Mason
and sent him reeling backwards into the wall. What an
arrogant jerk! "Listen here, Mason. You'd better give
Charisma up. I know she's nothing more to you than arm
candy and a pretty woman who might be a trophy wife
and hang on every word you utter. She deserves more

than that. She's brilliant, funny, so kind, and incredibly sexy..." I didn't have to say another word, because I watched as Mason's face grew dark with jealousy. I'd got him.

"Why Callum, you surprise me. You sound like a man in love."

"I am. I care so deeply for Charisma that I'd walk away from everything—even this just to have her. That's how much I love her. I would treat her like a queen, and be her servant. So, Mr. CEO, the question is, would you ever do that? I doubt it."

"So, you're saying that if I step back, you'll give up your rightful position as heir to Beast Company?" Mason asked.

I saw his eyes come alive with calculated plans and measures, practically drooling at the idea. "I would just to have her. How about you, little brother, would you?"

Mason didn't answer me, but he didn't need to. He thought I was unobservant and stupid, not business savvy, but I knew more than he thought I did. Money spoke with my brother way more than anything else, and I was going to use that to my advantage.

Chapter 18

Mason

I would never admit it to him, but Callum's challenge had given me some interesting food for thought. When push came to shove, did I really have the potential to put a relationship above business? I wasn't entirely certain about it, and I had no idea if I could really love Charisma enough to do that, because she did deserve that. However, not with Callum, damn it! He was no good for her and he may be trying to change now, but there was no way that he'd changed that much in such a short amount of time. I didn't buy it. But what was his game? Maybe he was just stupid enough to buy his own sales pitch.

What had been made quite clear was that a competition was on for her affections, Beast against Beast. Who would win? Frankly, Charisma probably deserved better than either of us with how we were being

so possessive of her, but she was just too exquisite and
beautiful to not see it through and seriously evaluate the
long term potential. A woman like that just didn't come
around every day—smart with business and life, as well
as tied together in a pretty package. I wanted her…badly,
especially after our weekend together on Catalina. It hit
me hard the morning after I had a taste of her. I was in
love with her. I didn't want to scare her off or pressure
her so soon after to go all the way with me the next night
so I held back, which wasn't typical of me. I'd never hold
back on getting what I wanted, but with Charisma, I was
scared. I was scared to make the wrong move.

Callum said that if he had Charisma that'd he'd
treat her like a queen. I'll admit, I felt a bit deceived by
Charisma, not letting me know that they'd grown as close
as they had. Had she been playing both of us? If she had,
she'd done a good job. That just didn't make sense,
though. She seemed different than that. I also thought, if
she really loved me and wanted to be with me, would she
expect me to choose her over business? Would she ever
be able to choose me over her mother's business? These
questions remained unanswered no matter how much I

delved into them, and I wanted to find out the truth. I had to know, and more importantly, I had to get her away from Callum before he sabotaged me in some way.

I picked up my phone and pulled up Charisma's contact information.

Me: Charisma, hi beautiful, how are you?

I knew she had a busy day, but I hoped that she was available just enough to get my text. I waited for what seemed like an eternity, but was only five minutes in real time.

Charisma: Hi there. I'm great—busy—how about you?

Me: Thinking of you. Wondering if you were available tonight? I'd love to take you to dinner.

Charisma: Sure, that would be great. What time?

Me: I'll pick you up at 7, if that works.

Charisma: No, I'll be downtown at a meeting, where can I meet you?

Me: Flash. Know where it is?

Charisma: Yes, see you then. Have to run.

All these unwelcomed second guesses flooded my mind, thanks to Callum and his unwelcomed visit. Was she really at a meeting downtown or did she just not want me to pick her up at her home and have Callum see? If that was the case, I had a bigger challenge on my hands than I'd thought I did. Well, I had to put it out of my mind, because that night I had to do something very important, seemingly urgent now. I had to see if Charisma and I truly had potential and if she was someone that I could put above all else and love unconditionally.

I loved Beast Company with this commitment that was hard to explain to someone, especially someone who didn't have a family business that they were excited about seeing live on through them, and becoming a part of their legacy. I'd always felt that way about the business and it had consumed me, but the second I saw Charisma, a part of me that I didn't know existed was also consumed. I lusted after her and craved her completely—from her smile to her smart comebacks to our talks about meaningful topics, not just shallow things.

***

Not able to concentrate, I'd arrived at the restaurant early, making sure that Charisma and I could secure a table in a quiet back corner. I wanted her all to myself and to have nothing interrupt our time together from the moment I saw her on. I felt nervous, too, hoping that the right words would just come to me on that night. It felt like so much was riding on it and I knew it was pressure I'd put on myself, but I was just overrun with desire, both for Charisma the person and Charisma the physical object.

Enjoying a martini to take the edge off, I had my back to the bar so I could keep an eye on the front door of the restaurant. At 7 PM precisely, Charisma walked in, looking drop dead gorgeous. She was wearing chic straight black pants, a black lace top and flat pointed shoes, which was unusual, but the way she carried herself made me feel like a bit of drool might escape the corner of my mouth. She was my prey and I was a savage beast. But she was limping?

I waved and walked right over to her.

"What's wrong? Are you okay?" I asked, placing my hand on her elbow as I reached down and kissed her cheek. I lingered there for a moment, intoxicated by her inviting scent.

"I twisted my ankle yesterday, but I'm fine. It's just a bit tender, especially after being on it all day," Charisma said, kissing my right cheek. Her hair brushed against me, making me feel like I'd been kissed by a seductive wind.

The woman could probably seal any deal she wanted to in life just by looks alone and I wasn't so sure that I'd be an exception to that rule.

"Well, would you rather eat at my apartment?" I asked. If she would have said yes I would not have complained.

"No, don't be silly. I'm starving, anyway," she said. She looked at me and smiled and I was so drawn in, but also filled with questions. If there would have been a tasteful and tactful way to do it, I would have grilled her about Callum, but there wasn't. So, I'd just have to focus on our undeniable chemistry and see where it took me.

I glanced over at the maitre de, who was looking at me waiting for the sign we were ready to sit, and I nodded my head. He guided came over and said, "Follow me, please."

I gestured for Charisma to go first and couldn't help but smile at how cute her strut looked with that slight limp. It made her beautiful heart shaped ass sway back and forth a bit more, almost exaggerated, but still highly appealing.

Once we sat down, we quickly ordered and then I had her to myself. I was so excited to indulge in her. I laughed at how she fell into the lake and tried to hide my frown that Callum had been there to lift her out of it, and that he'd even gone off somewhere with her mother. What was he pulling? My instincts told me that he was trying some clever ploy to sabotage me as CEO, but I couldn't focus on what that might be at that moment. Honestly, I didn't want to, either, because I just wanted to focus on the one thing I had control of—my time with Charisma at that moment.

"How's your paper coming along?" I asked. "I want to be as accommodating as possible and ensure you have everything you need."

"It's fantastic, actually. I have all the data and hope to turn in an initial draft to my teacher in about a week. Hard to believe my time there is almost done," she said.

"It doesn't have to be. You're bright and intelligent, everyone is drawn to you, I'm sure we can figure something out," I offered quickly.

"I can't be at two companies full time at once," Charisma said to me, smiling.

I reached out and touched her long, slender fingers, wanting to entwine my fingers with hers. I held back. "I suppose your mother would be most annoyed at me if I tried to steal you away. We could use someone with your discretionary eye to head up some new marketing campaigns."

"That's very kind, but you know that's not necessarily true, Mason," she said. "My specialty is business and topics that would actually make me better suited to compete with you for CEO."

She was playful when she said it, but it was true. "Everyone seems to want my job today."

"What do you mean?" Charisma asked.

"Oh nothing, just thinking out loud. It's tough to be the CEO, others like the thought of targeting you and making your job their job."

"Well, I wouldn't do that. I much rather prefer the challenge of making the Chu new money become our future generation's old money," Charisma teased.

"Touché," I said. I raised my wine glass and Charisma met me with hers. Then we both drank and caught the unavoidable look in each other's eyes. She was filled with a consuming desire that was easily spotted and I wanted to be the man to fulfill it. Maybe tonight we'd go further than that night on Catalina.

"What do you say we go someplace else for dessert?" I asked.

"Any place special in mind?" she asked, smiling at me seductively and flirtatiously.

"I have an idea," I said.

"Then what are we waiting for, Mason."

***

I pulled the Range Rover into the garage and walked around to the passenger door to open it up and help Charisma out of the passenger seat. Just from her touch I felt this excitement generate through me and felt that it would be all I could do to maintain my control, to control myself until the time was right. This night had to be perfect, as beautifully coordinated as an orchestra pit that was building up to the crescendo during their signature piece of their performance.

Charisma smiled at me and I could only smile back, thinking, *you make me believe that I could do things I otherwise thought impossible.* Even two months ago, if someone told me I may be willing to put business, especially the family business, behind any one person or situation, I wouldn't have believed it. Yet there I was, seriously considering it.

"So, this is your beach condo?" she asked, looking at me and not hiding her surprise.

"It is, my place to retreat and get away from it all. I don't take people here too often," I said.

"No, why not?" she asked.

"Some may call it my man-cave, I guess, but it's a place where all the things that are important to me—things that are often put to the side now—can be and I can come and visit, recharging my batteries and taking advantage of relaxing if I get the chance."

"That's a great idea—every CEO should have one of these," Charisma said, smiling and hooking her arm through mine. I opened up the service door and we entered in on the lower level, which had large glass doors that led out to the beach and then onto the ocean.

Against the one wall were a few of my surfboards, on pegs so they could be used as decorations when they weren't in use from me. It was prime surfing real estate, which I got to use far too seldom.

"You surf?" she asked.

I laughed at her shock. "Don't sound so shocked, Charisma. I surf. In fact, I would every day if my life allowed for it. How about you?"

"I surf some, but not too much. I'm not the most graceful when my footing is not on solid ground." Then she laughed and pointed to her ankle, adding, "Case in point."

"Well, maybe I could give you some tips sometime," I said. "Let me show you upstairs."

As we made our way up the winding staircase to the main level, she continued on. "How long have you owned this?"

"Since college," I said. "I'd used a small set of inheritance for me from my grandfather to purchase it." I wasn't sure why I felt the need to disclose that, but I did.

"Well, it was probably a good investment. Property is hard to come by in this area, isn't it?"

"I forget how you're as smart as you are beautiful," I said, looking at her. My hand lifted up to her face and touched her soft, silky cheek.

"I'd like to think I'm smarter," she said, blushing slightly.

"Well, whatever you are, it's quite perfect to me," I replied.

Then we walked onto the main level and Charisma looked around as I gave her a tour. Modern kitchen with stainless steel, a balcony that went to the outside and gave an even better view of the ocean, a bathroom, two bedrooms—one a master, and a cozy living room with a fireplace in the center.

"So amazing," Charisma said, walking out onto the balcony after I slid open the glass doors that led to it on that side. "The view is truly breathtaking, Mason."

"It is," I said, "but this isn't the best view. That's on the third floor. Come."

I grabbed her hand and started to guide her up the last set of spiral stairs, which were truly my stairway to heaven in a way. "This spot is my favorite in this condo. The reason I brought it, really."

"Ooh, I'm intrigued then, because this place is pretty amazing thus far."

Once we made it to the top floor, Charisma looked around and her mouth was slightly open. I could see her chest moving in and out slightly, breathing as rhythmically as the ocean waves were lapping up onto the shore outside.

Beautiful Girl: Modern Beauty and Beast (Happy Ever After Standalone Novel Series)

This place was my sanctuary. It had a bookshelf wall that was filled with all of my favorite books, both business and fiction. I loved the classics, the stories that defined people's paths and shaped their future. My telescope was right in the center, pointed up toward Jupiter, the last planet that I'd been observing when it had come into sight, and my painting supplies were on the right side. An easel with a blank canvass was set up, but it was blank, a hundred shades of paints nearby in their small tubes, and all the supplies organized on the table.

"You surf. You paint. I never would have guessed," Charisma said. She walked over to the easel and her fingers reached out and she softly brushed it as if they were a paint brush.

"I used to devote a lot of time to these things, until…until I had to make a decision between the family business and these hobbies. Callum wasn't really…" My words trailed off, because I didn't want to talk about him.

"You really take pride in your family's achievements, don't you?" she asked. The way she looked at me showed this shocked tenderness in her eyes that made her even more beautiful—something I wouldn't have thought was possible. It made her breathtaking to me.

"I do, and I can tell you do, as well. I admire that about you. A family is who you connect with, whether large or small," I said. Really, I felt like my family was just Mother and me now, finding it challenging to include Callum. I still had so much anger festering in me toward him and didn't know if I could ever trust him, or fully forgive him.

"You should find time to do this stuff more," Charisma said in response, her hand gesturing to all the things in this room. "Never forget who you are."

"You talk like a wise old soul," I said, walking over to her and putting my hands on her shoulders. I was right behind her and wanted to cradle my arms around her so much they ached.

Beautiful Girl: Modern Beauty and Beast (Happy Ever After Standalone Novel Series)

"I listen to my mother," she said, laughing softly and then she shocked me and turned around, pressing her lips against mine.

Our bodies latched together, our kisses were our permission to each other to go wherever we wanted on each other's body. I guided her over to the daybed, which was in the room and the place I most often slept when I stayed at the condo. Before she went onto it, she began to peel her clothes off fearlessly and seductively, maintaining eye contact with me the entire time. "The way you made me feel the other night, Mason. I can't forget about it," she said honestly.

I moaned, watching her naked beautiful body show itself as she sat down on the daybed. Her hands went to my hips and she moved me closer and began to undo my pants and slide them down, whispering, "Let me."

She moved slowly and methodically, seeming to appreciate every movement for what it was and staring at me like I was a piece of art in a museum. Such attention and thought, it was so selfless and loving.

Then there we were, naked with a slight ocean breeze coming in the window of the loft area. I could not take my eyes off her. She was the finest piece of art I'd ever seen. So exquisite, so beautiful. Looking at her, I could not help but want her, to take her, to possess her. Yet I also wanted to take care of her, make love to her, to make her happy, and to cherish her.

"I want you so bad, Charisma; it's been killing me," I said as I leaned over her, kissing her neck with my heated breath. I could feel my large erect bulge touching against the smooth skin of her taut stomach.

"I want you too," she said.

"Let me be the first," I whispered. "Let me please you."

"Mason, you're not..." My mind started to feel heavy and I knew what she's said, but it turned my tenderness into something more animalistic and savage.

Beautiful Girl: Modern Beauty and Beast (Happy Ever After Standalone Novel Series)

She'd given Callum her virginity! How could she do that? I didn't know, but I knew that I wanted to pound her so hard that she forgot about Callum or that he even existed. I wanted the mark of my attraction to her to be so undeniably strong that she wouldn't be able to wipe it from her face. She'd have the look of a woman who'd been sexually pleasured and pushed to the brink of her desires, leaving her believing she could never have better, while also longing for more.

Yes, I was jealous and I was angry, and I took it out in aggressiveness that showed her how much I wanted to do to her and how intense those feelings were. As I bit at her beautiful nipples, tugging at them like I was a lion eating the prey that would sustain me another day, I kept going and going. My fingers made her wetter, my hands found every spot that stimulated her on her body and pressed all the right buttons. With each gasp, moan, and whisper of my name I became more adrenalized and so did she. Then I slid into her, moving back and forth, opening my eyes to see her back arched and her chest heaving in excitement, screaming out my name louder and louder, her words only escaping out the open window. And then she orgasmed. It was beautiful and raw, her sounds guttural. As I watched her beautiful display of pleasure, I found myself releasing into her, feeling the heat of our liquids colliding like lava might clash with the cold air that existed outside of it. And afterward, I collapsed onto her, my lips by her ears and murmuring, "Incredible."

The voices in my mind were strong as I stayed so close to her, the heat of our bodies gluing us together, and I realized just how torn I was. Beast Companies or her was a huge decision, and I wasn't sure it was one that had to be made, but if that's what I was pitted against due to Callum's manipulation, I just might have to. Our sex had been perfect, our bodies understanding each other's needs, and emotionally, I felt so alive and connected when we spoke. There were very few women who appealed to me that way—none as much as Charisma, either.

I finally rolled to my side and onto my elbow, gently blowing on her lovely flesh, and asked, "Do you want me as much as I want you?"

"Yes," she said. There was no hesitation and she sounded confident in her words, which made me so happy. I knew now I was completely in love with her.

"Good, please stay tonight," I said. Before she could answer, I wanted to physically show her why there was no better choice than me. Being with me was her best option.

Chapter 19

Callum

Charisma had never come home after work and I knew that there was one logical explanation for it—Mason. He'd gotten to her and it brought me physical pain, almost worst than after the accident, because it was my heart and mind, agonizing with how much I missed her and intensely pounding out the message that I wanted to experience her physically again and continue to show her the amazing world of sex when someone who loved you unconditionally and completely gave themselves to you.

I debated giving her a call, but resisted. I wasn't sure why, but I just couldn't do it. I didn't want to be overly controlling or possessive; I just wanted to love her...again and again. This was so crazy! And I'd never felt so vulnerable and so nervous about my life than this, and it was made worst by the tormented thoughts of

Beautiful Girl: Modern Beauty and Beast (Happy Ever After Standalone Novel Series)

Charisma being with Mason. *My brother*, I sneered. He'd made me out to be a monster to her, taking bits of truth from the old me and making them sound like they were the only me. I was changed!

I shouldn't have thrown that offer down about turning over Beast Companies to him, I thought. I had only said it because I didn't believe he'd ever be able to do that. It wasn't part of who he was and unlike me, Mason couldn't ever put business to the side to give a woman like Charisma the relationship she deserved. Yet, my arrogance had set me up for this moment, in a way, but damn it, I'd only done it out of love.

Staring up at the ceiling from my bed, I glanced over at my clock. 11 PM. Then midnight, and then finally, I heard the front door open. Should I go greet her, or wait? I couldn't wait. I was driving myself crazy.

In my shorts and with no shirt on, I walked into the living room and saw her there, trying to be quiet and her hair looking wild. She had the look of a woman who'd been loved and it killed me. It was a good thing that

Mason wasn't there, because I didn't think I could control myself if he was. But I had to be calm. "Charisma," I said.

She looked up, her eyes traveling right toward me and she smiled. "Callum," she replied simply.

"I'm glad you're home. I missed you," I said. I had to be honest here and not play games. I had to remember that this woman was a free spirit and independent, not just a prize, but she had to know that how I felt was genuine, that what I'd said the night before was sincere.

"Sorry, I guess I should have called," she said in a whisper, glancing over at the large clock in the corner.

"You don't owe me anything. I'm just glad to see you," I said. I walked over to her and grabbed her hand. "I want to talk with you. Can we go out into the backyard for a few minutes?"

"Sure," she said. I still felt the energy in our touch, just like I had, and I prayed that it was strong enough that

she could feel it through whatever trance Mason may
have put on her. "I wanted to talk with you, too."

We were out in the backyard and sat down on a
small bench that was near a fountain, the moonlight now
glimmering on the ocean water in the distance. The air
was slightly chilly, but the energy was so intense that I
wasn't cold, and I saw that Charisma wasn't either.

"What did you want to say?" I asked.

"Please, you go first," she said. "You've been
waiting a long time I think." Her voice was gentle and
kind.

"What I told you last night, I meant," I said
directly. "Charisma, I love you so much and no matter
what else I'd have to give up, or what I may have to do to
prove it, I'm willing to. I just want to be with you and
make you my queen and give you everything I can. The
only thing I require from you is that you love me. Can you
ever do it? Love a damaged man like me?"

"Callum, don't you realize that it's clear to see that you've changed. And I believe you have genuinely changed, that it's not just an act."

"But the scars…"

She put her fingers gently on my lips, quieting me down. "No," and then she leaned in and gave me a soft, tender kiss that felt closer to genuine love than any kiss I'd ever received. Afterward, she said, "You are so beautiful, Callum. The scars, they're barely visible. If you only look, you'd see that, and even if they were, it's the man inside that I'm most drawn to."

"You are?" I asked, feeling my empty insides filling up with hope.

She softly said, "Yes." Then she rested her head into the crook of my arm and we were silent. I felt connected to her in a magical way, wanting to take advantage of this moment of silence, because in the unspoken words, a volume about the potential of our love was being expressed.

**Beautiful Girl: Modern Beauty and Beast (Happy Ever
After Standalone Novel Series)**

Chapter 20

Callum

I stood there, exhilarated and scared, not knowing how to process the intensity of this woman who made me feel like I'd never felt before. She was so good and kind, unlike any woman my age I'd ever met. She'd had a wonderful example through her mother, but she was a rare gift—equally as beautiful on the inside as she was on the out.

Watching her closely and breathing in, I noticed her compassionate face turn into one with an eager smile on it. "Come," she said, grabbing my hand and turning around to walk back into the house.

I followed, eager to do whatever it was she wanted me to do. I trusted her implicitly and she gave me hope, something I needed desperately.

A few seconds later, we were standing in front of an ornate full length mirror in the foyer of the house, a pedestal with fresh cut flowers next to it, and she turned on a lamp that was nearby, making light instantly flood into the room. Then she stood behind me, her hands on my arms and her head peeking around my left side so she could watch me through the mirror. I looked at her and smiled, nervous to look at anything else. I'd once worshipped a mirror, but after the accident I avoided them as much as I could.

"Look at yourself," she gently said, encouraging me with her tender voice.

I was hesitant, but I did. She didn't say a word, but her touch gave me courage. I glanced into the mirror and gave a long, slow blink. I didn't want to see what I'd become.

"Callum, just look," Charisma said in an even softer voice.

I wanted to, but I couldn't. "No," I said, feeling such anxiety inside of me that I shuttered involuntarily from it.

"It's okay, Callum. You are beautiful. Look and tell me what you see—actually what you do not see," she whispered.

I could only nod my head and then I leaned forward and forced myself to be strong and look at me. Maybe I'd be able to see what Charisma did. With a critical and assessing eye, I stared at myself. The lighting must have been poor because I could barely see the scars on my face. It was a bit of the old me, only with wiser eyes. I leaned in closer and looked again, this time tilting my head and pressing my hands where the scars were. I could barely feel them, either.

"You see, they're almost gone. They're healed," Charisma said, a large infectious smile spreading across her face.

"Gone," I replied, a question clearly in my voice, along with disbelief.

"Yes, gone," she said, rubbing her soft long hands along my arms, filling me up with her kindness and love.

So much had changed inside of me since that accident, as well as externally. It was overwhelming and I was so appreciative, realizing how fortunate I was to have encountered both Helen and Charisma. Without them, this wouldn't be. And furthermore, without the Helen Chu Cosmetics Miracle Cream this wouldn't have happened. Everything that I'd so willingly snickered at and slammed on that one fateful night had been what had saved me in the end. But somehow, the universe had forgiven me when I couldn't forgive myself, and my karma had led me to a miraculous spot—the place where I was with who I wanted to be with and feeling this internal harmony that I would have thought was more mythological than anything.

"Don't you see, you're amazing, whole on the outside and inside, too," Charisma said. Her voice was so affectionate that I felt the sting of tears in my eyes. She'd affected me so intensely that I couldn't even explain it. Did other people feel these same thing? I had no idea, but it was a beautiful feeling—a gateway into a new and improved world where people treated each other lovingly and really cared.

"So what do you think of Helen Chu Cosmetics now?" I turned around and saw Helen walking over to the mirror, a gentle and wise smile on her face.

"I think you're a miracle maker," I said, laughing. It felt so good to genuinely laugh at that moment and celebrate that I'd been given a second chance, both as a man and with a different appreciation for physical beauty.

"I look at you and see a young and confident man, but a smarter man. You are so different than the Callum Beast I first met," Helen said.

"Thank goodness, because that man was not good. I want to be good," I acknowledged.

"Oh Callum, you've changed so much, right before our very eyes. I meet both men and women all the time, that feel a need to connect with their inner beauty just as much as their outward appearance. In only a few short months, you've managed to transform in an incredible way and now you're ready for the next step," Helen said.

I looked at her in confusion. "What do you mean?"

"It's time you re-entered the world and went back to your family to make things right. That's what you promised your father and I know that you will want to honor that," Helen said.

It was a cautionary statement, but also meant to encourage me. "Are you saying it's time for me to go?"

Helen walked up to me and grabbed my hand in hers and said, "I'm saying it's time you go back to your own house, own family, and step into the shoes you were supposed to fill, Callum."

"So, I've overstayed my welcome," I said. I felt so sad by it, never having put any thought into this day, because I'd loved being here so much, but I knew that Helen was right.

"Not overstayed, but I would be doing you a great disservice if I didn't encourage you to go do what you're meant to do, Callum."

I looked at Charisma and feigned cheeriness. Despite being happy about the scars just seconds ago, I felt scared and a bit of a void inside of me at the thought of not seeing these two amazing women every day. "Help me pack, Charisma?"

"Of course," she said softly. When our eyes connected I saw sadness in her eyes that seemed to match what I was feeling. Did she not want me to go? The thought gave me hope that I could claim a woman like Charisma's heart when all was said and done.

***

As soon as we got to my temporary room I had to speak my mind. "I guess your mom doesn't want anything happening between us, huh."

"Why do you say that?" Charisma asked. I knew that she was smart enough to know.

"It seems obvious. At the festival she saw how connected we were and it's just a few days later, and now it's time for me to go."

"No, I don't think that's it; it can't be," Charisma said.

"You're being kind, but you can be honest with me. And really, whatever it is that your mother is thinking, I will respect her wishes. I admire her greatly and would never defy her, especially after all the help she's given—help that you've given, too."

Then I went and grabbed my two suitcases. It didn't take me long to pack and the entire time I was there I kept glancing at Charisma, who was sitting on the edge of the bed and watching me with keen eyes. But, when our eyes met she'd glance down, averting her gaze and protecting herself from exposing what she was really thinking. Was she relieved? Or was she sad? My heart longed for her to feel the same void I did at the thought of me leaving, but I didn't dare be so presumptuous.

One hour later, I was getting ready to leave.

"Callum, I'm going to miss you," she said softly, looking at her fingernails and then to me.

She stood up from the edge of the bed and I walked over to her and wrapped my arms around her, hugging her tightly. I had to tell her what was on my mind, less I never get the chance again. "I love you,

Charisma. Even if your mom doesn't want some kind of romance between us, I still care for you. I don't think that could ever stop, the journey has been too incredible. Being here with your mother and you have taught me so much, things that are a part of me now, that I'll never take away."

"Oh Callum," Charisma lamented.

I smiled and put my finger under her chin and continued. "Because of you two, I've learned to open my eyes and heart to people. You were instrumental in that and I owe you so much because of it, Charisma. You have no idea how you and your mom have given me a new lease on life."

Her arms wrapped around me tightly and she pressed her head into my chest. My arms went around her slim frame and I pulled her tighter into my chest. It brought me such comfort and I wanted to be a source of security for her, too. I longed for her to ask me to stay, because I wanted to, but I also realized that in order to hopefully become the man she deserved, that I'd have to enter this world and not be fearful of being Callum Beast. I'd have to prove that I'd changed and while it would be a tough battle, it would be a worthwhile battle, especially with her as the prize at the end of it all.

I needed to feel her again, to cement my passion for her on her in some way and I leaned in and kissed her fiercely and unabashedly, pressing my lips against hers and forcing my tongue into her mouth, wanting to taste her and experience her.

"So damn beautiful," I whispered.

She groaned and I felt my arousal growing. No! I had to stop. If my last moment with her was one where our bodies clashed together in the heat of passion it would distract me forever, making me an addict to her love, always longing for more and dreaming of that moment instead of living my life to its fullest potential.

It wasn't easy, but I pulled away and in a barely audible voice, I said, "Goodbye Charisma."

Then I turned around and walked away, not willing to look back and see what expression she might have.

Chapter 21

Charisma

Why did a part of me feel like it was being ripped out of me as I watched Callum leave? I wanted to chase him, but I didn't. I remained frozen in place, confused and startled by the situation I was in. It was so unfair and I didn't even know how to process my feelings.

Eventually, I did walk out of the empty guest room and over to my room. It was strange, when Callum had first arrived at our house I felt like our rooms were so close, but now, I felt like he was too far away when he was even out of eyesight. No one was more shocked than me at how quickly I'd gotten used to his presence—even longing for it and feeling better with it now.

You should have gone after him, I thought. But really, what would I say? I wasn't ready to say that I chose him and wanted him to stay, that I couldn't live without him. I felt like I loved him, but was I in love with him? I didn't know. And I didn't know those answers any better regarding Mason, either. But Mason and I, we were so alike. It was more logical, for certain, but equally certain was the awareness that logic was defying me at that moment. Damn it, I despised confusion and a lack of clarity, just as much in my business prowess as my personal life.

Flopped on my bed and feeling like a fish out of water, I stared up at the ceiling, watching the blades of my ceiling fan slowly spin around and around and around. It was hypnotic, but didn't bring answers. My cautious nature had always led to me avoiding situations that might bring me discomfort, agony, or heartache; partly because I saw how much Mom had been hurt from being abandoned by my father. That was why I never took my father's surname but used my mom's name instead. She'd never married again and only dated occasionally. So devoted to me and her work, she never tried to find love again. I didn't want to be that person, yet there I was, looking like I was playing two brothers, loving each of them clearly in different ways. Was it the type of love that meant a permanent commitment? I had no idea nor experience to have an inkling, and my friends who were always quite casual about sex, friends with benefits, and all those different modern notions didn't rattle easily.

There was a knock on the door and I barely turned my head to look at my mom standing there, her shoulder resting against the door frame. "Mind if I come in?" she asked.

"Sure," I said and then my eyes went back to the ceiling like it was interesting subject matter.

"Want to talk about it?" she asked.

Did I want to talk about it? Hmph...what was there to say? I was a mess of emotions and had no intellectual intelligence to process them. Finally, I asked the only question that I could think of. "Why *did* you ask Callum to leave?"

"Why do you think I did?" she asked.

"I don't' know, maybe to keep me from him," I offered. It wasn't my thought or belief, but Callum had thought that might be the case.

"You know that I'd never sabotage your happiness, Charisma, so no, if you're implying that I had him leave because you two were getting too close, you'd be wrong. But somehow, I don't think that's your idea, or thought."

"You know me well," I said, giving a weak smile.

"Yes, I do, but right now I'm looking at a young woman who understands life in business terms, not emotional ones."

"It's so hard. I can see why you never bothered after Dad abandoned us," I said.

"It wasn't that I didn't want to, but I got so wrapped up in everything. Finding success, taking care of you, raising you, and building a future that would ensure you had more security than I ever had. Maybe it was the wrong way—to some, anyway—but I don't regret it. I've actually found a life that suits me quite well."

"Do you think that you'll ever experience a loving relationship again?" I asked.

"I do, actually. Has it been my priority? No, but I firmly believe and have seen that love always arrives when it's least expected. I think you're perhaps experiencing that."

"Do you mean with Callum?" I asked.

"Maybe, or maybe with Mason. I don't know what's in your heart, Charisma."

"How do I figure it out?" I asked, feeling so vulnerable.

"Time will help, it always does, but there is one thing that I do know, regardless of which brother—if either—you decide is the one you're meant to be with."

Beautiful Girl: Modern Beauty and Beast (Happy Ever After Standalone Novel Series)

"What's that?" I asked, sitting up now and positioning my body so I was looking at her.

"I don't want to have to take care of him and you for the rest of my life. You kids need to grow up, go out and live your lives, and eventually start a family; not stay with me, constantly working and hiding and resisting the experiences that make life amazing. I love having you here, of course, but I also love the idea of having grandkids, seeing you marry a man who loves you wildly and takes great care of you, both emotionally and financially. The thought of me having a son-in-law that I have to take care of doesn't sit well with me, at all. And if Callum can't step up to become a man who can run Beast Companies; then he won't be the man who can handle you."

"Mom!" I exclaimed. "We are nowhere close to anything like that. We haven't even dated."

"But I see how you two are, it's not dates that make a connection, it's the way people interact with each other that does. There is something fascinating there, to be certain, but I also see fascination elsewhere." I looked at Mom and her eyes twinkled. "And Mason, he's a gentleman and he's already up and running, doing a very good job from what others tell me, including you. I look at him and I know with absolute certainty that he's a man who can take care of you."

"So you think I should date him and forget about Callum?" I asked. I'll admit, I hoped that she'd give me an answer and I could just listen to her like an obedient small child and make it all work out.

"I would never answer that question for you, even if I had a strong opinion," Mom said. She put her hand on my knee. "But you have to be confident to answer it. Chu women don't shy or back away from large tasks."

"It seems larger than the universe itself," I said, laughing a bit.

"That's because love fills the universe just as the debris in it seems to gravitate toward our minds, Charisma."

"That's very poetic," I said.

"Poetic words from my wise grandmother, a woman who'd never had a day of formal education in her life," Mom said. "I guess I want you to have an education that makes you as smart with your heart as you are with your head."

"I would give anything for that," I said.

"I know, and it will all work out in due time—maybe not your time, but in the right time, Charisma."

Then she got up and I followed suit, giving her a warm embrace. "Thanks, Mom. You always know what to say."

"That's sweet of you to say, but I don't know if my words will help. It's how you act and the choices you make that will really determine the outcome of this story."

Kailin Gow

Chapter 22

Charisma

And then my life moved on. Although I was done at Beast Companies, I continued to see Mason. He was good, kind and a philanthropist who treated me like a queen.

I hadn't even had the chance to talk to Callum or see him. Since leaving our house and work, I haven't heard from him for weeks. He didn't return my calls or emails either so I thought he didn't want to see me again, especially the way we parted.

Perhaps he was avoiding me, but in his absence, there left an uncluttered room for my heart and mind to embrace a possible future with Mason. He'd hint at things, but at first I was hesitant to accept them, believing that they may be the result of some type of competition with Callum. However, that suspicion diminished rapidly whenever Mason would look at me. There was no denying his love for me when I saw the true look of love in his eyes.

With each passing day spent with Mason, the more our relationship grew. But I still couldn't stop caring about Callum and how he was doing.

One day I asked Mason, "Is everything going well with Callum back home?" I asked. I'd wanted to sound casual, but wasn't entirely certain I had.

I felt Mason's body stiffen up. "Why would you ask that?" he asked. He turned to me and his eyes looked hard and calculating—his defenses were up.

"I was just curious. I haven't heard from him."

"Does that bother you?" he asked, staring at me even more closely.

"No, but I just want him to be okay. Hopefully you do, too."

"I have to tell you, I really don't know. He decided to get a place downtown and not move back home," Mason said. Then he added, "Mother helped him pay for it."

"Oh," I said. Then I dropped it, because it was clearly a controversial topic with Mason. Plus, I realized the insensitivity of my timing. Wrapped up in each other's arms, after a romantic evening that ended in passionate sex, and Mason knowing full well that his brother had taken my virginity—something I was certain Mason would have cherished, I should've asked about Callum another time. But in the back of my mind, I was impressed with Callum's actions, as it took courage and tenacity, two qualities I greatly admired to start life all over again…to go from rock bottom and try to climb back to the top.

And although he told me he loved me and would fight for me, Mason was always around me, taking care of my every needs, and becoming closer and closer to me.

Nights of making love until midnight were common for Mason and I. It was both beautiful and intense sometimes animalistic helping us to release the wild side of us and letting us feel unrestrained, uninhibited yet free. We both needed each other for it, getting the release we crave from the stresses of life.

I'd awake every morning with a sweet text message from Mason, which made me smile, and then I'd respond, trying to tap into the beautiful words of wisdom my mother so often said, but put a business twist on them. It was something that was utterly Mason and I in most every way, but likely not someone else's idea of romance. We had an exciting fusion that was filled with intense passion, an insatiable appetite for business, endless innovative ideas, and a natural determination that would not be hindered.

And I still haven't heard from Callum so it was time to move on. Or so I thought.

Chapter 23

Callum

It had been heartbreaking not getting in contact with Charisma all these months. But I needed to step away from her so I could focus on winning the trust and confidence of the Board for the Beast Company.

It was also a condition Mason and I agreed on so that I could come onboard and back into the Beast Company. Mason didn't trust me with Charisma, thinking I was still that shallow idiot I was long ago. I didn't want to agree to his terms at first, but then I realized it was because he was trying to protect Charisma from me. He had a point after all since I was the one who hurled insults towards her mother and her long ago.

Plus, Mason wanted to see how serious I was in rebuilding the Beast's family name as well as the Beast

Company's reputation. Any mention of my name with Helen Chu and even Charisma Chu in the media or social media would bring up the awful accident again. So I agreed to that term along with the Board's votes in order for me to get reinstated onto the Board itself.

Then as the months went by, and I realized that Mason was taking full advantage of my inability to get in touch with Charisma, by getting closer and closer to her; I was heartbroken, first and foremost, but then something inside of me turned that into inspiration. I wasn't the type of man she needed, and I could accept that, but she was just the type of woman I desired. That meant that I had to find a way to tap into the business side of me that Mason so naturally possessed, and show that I had it in me, too.

It was the biggest sacrifice I could make, but I knew deep down inside Charisma and Helen would be proud of me for doing it. My father would be proud of me for it.

"Mason," I walked into his office.

Mason turned around from facing the window in his office. "What is it?"

"It's been 6 months. Do you think I am capable of running Beast's Stores now?"

"We'll let the Board determine that," Mason said. "But from my record, they would probably want to keep things status quo and have me remain CEO."

"We'll see," I said. "And I'll break my terms with you on keeping away from Charisma."

Mason clenched his fist. "Like I said, we'll let the Board decide. But as far as Charisma is concern, she and I are very much in love. I won't give her up without a fight."

"I'll fight you then, Mason. I know she cared about me once…"

Mason walked up to me so fast and pulled me forward. I have never seen him so angry and emotional.

"You touch her or kiss her, then you're dead meat. You
hear."

I smiled. I knew I had him then. "So, Mason,
remember that bet I made with you months ago. If you
step down as CEO for Charisma, I promise to not interfere
with you and Charisma. But if you mistreat her in any
way, the bet's off."

Mason laughed. "I'm not threatened by you over
Charisma. I know she loves me, as much as I love her. I
don't need to give up my position to have her."

I couldn't help holding back my feelings then. To
hear Charisma in love with Mason was like a punch in the
stomach. But then again, it was coming from Mason
himself. Of course he would think Charisma loved him.
They weren't married yet.

"Fine, I'm going to invite her out to dinner with
me tonight," I said. "I miss her, and I'm sure she missed
me. After all, she chose me to give her virginity to, didn't
she? She must've cared for me a lot to do that."

At that, Mason punched me in the face, while I staggered back. Mason truly loved Charisma for him to lose control like that at the office.

"You try to seduce her again, and I will personally kill you," Mason said.

"That's for her to decide, isn't it?" I said wiping my jaw. The guy can throw a punch. Who knew he was that strong. "Worried?"
Mason didn't answer for a moment.

I pulled out my phone and began calling Charisma. To her credit, she answered right away.

"Hi Charisma," I said. My heart was pounding so hard as I wait to hear her voice again. How was she? What was she up to? I had so many questions to ask her.

"Callum?" she asked. "Is it really you? Oh God," she sound like she was crying. "I thought something happened to you. You never returned my emails or calls. Are you alright?"

"I'm fine," I said. "I'm working at Beast's Stores now, and doing well. I had the best teachers in you and your mother, Charisma." I tried to hold my longing for her as I talked to her. Just her voice had awakened my love and desire for her. I wanted so badly to tell her I love her, but Mason grabbed my phone.

"Hi Baby," he said. "It's me Mason. Yes, Callum is in the office with me. Why didn't I tell you he was working at Beast's Stores? Well, that was for him to tell you, right Callum, seeing that you'd rather avoid any contact with Charisma so you can get back into Beast Stores."

Mason handed me the phone and put Charisma on speaker. "Isn't that true, Callum?" he asked.

"Callum," Charisma said. "Is it true you wanted to severe all ties to me and Mom just to return back to Beast's? Why? What does that mean? Did all that time you lived with us mean nothing to you?"

My heart fell as I heard the hurt and anguish in Charisma's voice.

"Isn't it true, Callum," Mason goaded.

I took a deep breath and said, "I'm sorry, Charisma, it was true."

"I'm sorry to hear that," Charisma said coldly. "I see where your values are. I wished I never…" she broke off.

I spoke into the phone, ignoring Mason, as I poured my heart out. "Charisma, believe me, you and your mother meant everything to me. Everything between us was true. I owe my becoming a more mature man, being changed to someone who can gain the trust of the Board again all to you and Helen."

"How could you ignore my calls to you then?" Charisma asked. "You don't turn your back to those who cared about you."

Mason flinched when she said "cared."

"I'm doing this for you and Helen," I said. "I want you both to be proud of me," I said.

"We are, Callum, but you don't have to forget us for it."

"If I could," I began, looking at Mason. "I would give up the CEO position at Beast's Company…"

Mason grabbed my phone and turned off the speaker before I could finish my sentence. "Baby," he said. "If Callum became CEO of Beast's, would you dump me and start dating him?"

I couldn't hear her response since Mason was now talking quietly with Charisma on the phone. But he sounded completely like a lovelorn puppy. He was changed. Smiling as he talked on the phone with Charisma, while saying, "I love you so much, Baby. I will…anything for you." Then he hung up the phone and handed it to me.

"So Mason, should I call Charisma to ask her to dinner with me tonight?" I asked.

"I can't keep you from calling her," Mason said. "But I can tell you, she just said yes to marrying me."

My heart fell like a brick, and I felt like I needed to sit down. Mason just took the wind out of my sails.

"On the condition that I give you a chance with the Board to be voted in as CEO," Mason said.

My heart lifted a bit, thinking Charisma really did still care for me.

"Which I agreed to," Mason said. "And if the Board votes you in as CEO, then I'll accept that."

I was torn. I was happy that Mason relented to have me get a chance to become CEO, but heartbroken that I had just lost the love of my life.

Chapter 24

<u>Callum</u>

Walking into the board room a few days later was nerve wracking and exciting. I had so much to prove, much of what I had to demonstrate to them, but also a great deal more that I had to demonstrate to no one other than me.

"Gentlemen, hello, and thank you," I said, walking into the board room upon the invitation from the receptionist.

"Callum, you're looking well," they all said in various forms. I looked at Mason and he was sitting there with a poker face on. What he was really thinking, I had no idea, but he wasn't the one to decide if I could resume the role of CEO. The remainder of the board was. I was up against a big obstacle, because Mason had done very well in the position, showing business savvy and personal skills that were definitely indicators to show that he was also my father's son.

"Thank you," I said, acknowledging each of them with a handshake. "It was a rough few months, but I've never been better as a result. I'm driven, focused, and appreciative of everything it takes to be a Beast who can run Beast Companies and represent our time honored traditions in a way that my father and even grandfather would have been proud of."

They looked to Mason to take the lead. "How has your knowledge of all the workings of the company been increased, Callum? Not just the marketing department and modeling."

It was a fair question and I went on to explain. Over the past months, I'd taken it upon myself to also hire a personal mentor to help me tap into my potential and I was relieved and excited to realize that it had been a lack of desire that had been holding me back, a refusal to grow up. Well, I had grown up and have become smarter and wiser than I had ever been. I was ready.

Over the next hour, I laid out my plans for what I envisioned, showing I was ready to take over, including the smartest, logical choice to emulate my father, which was to keep Mason on as COO and also bring in Charisma to work for the company. Unbeknownst to her, I'd approached Helen with this idea, wanting to clear it through her. I had so much respect for that woman and all she'd done for me that I would never do something that might be misconstrued as deceitful. She'd given her blessings, though, reminding me that it was Charisma's choice, and hers alone to make. If she did take the job it might be tough at times, because I still loved her dearly and felt she was the right one for me. However, it wasn't our destiny, as evidenced by her and Mason's new engagement.

"Callum, can you give us a few moments," Mason asked.

"Certainly."

"It won't be long," he added.

I walked out and took a seat just outside the boardroom. I'd done the best I could and now it was in the hands of the men and women behind those thick, heavy wooden doors. Would Mason try to sabotage me or realize that it was time and the position was still supposed to be mine? I had to hope for the best, as the new man I wanted to be would only look at his opposition as a roadblock, not a dead end.

About twenty minutes later, I was brought back into the room, and everyone was standing up to shake my hand and congratulate me, including Mason. We patted each other's backs and I said, "Thank you for your vote of confidence and support."

"You're welcome, brother. I have all I need and more. That's what I want for you, too," he replied. I looked at him to assess the sincerity and his smile didn't quite reach his eyes, but he didn't look angry, either. A small step in the right direction, I supposed.

A month later...

Beautiful Girl: Modern Beauty and Beast (Happy Ever After Standalone Novel Series)

"Hi Callum, I'm not sure if you remember me. Veronica Chan, the winner of Miss Moon this past year. You took my photo, and Helen Chu Cosmetics were our sponsors."

"Yes, how could I forget. How is everything going with you, Veronica?" I asked.

"Very well, thanks. I'm starting med school in the fall at UCI actually, but I wanted to take advantage of us meeting before and see if you had any positions available that I might be qualified for."

"I can't imagine that we wouldn't have something available for an intelligent, beautiful and hard-working woman such as yourself. What did you have in mind?" She began to talk and while it was about work, it made something feel alive in me again. Maybe, just maybe, I was ready to move on and find a new opportunity for love.

Epilogue

Charisma

2 months later...

Mason and I sat across from each other in the chic restaurant Flash.

"I've been meaning to do this for a while, Charisma," Mason said, staring at me across the small table, the single candle flickering light that made his green eyes reflect its flame. "It's been so incredible, Charisma. You amaze me every day." He lifted his glass, the red wine shimmering in the soft ambiance, and I raised mine toward it and we toasted.

A waiter dressed in formal wear came by to deliver the dessert on a silver platter. On top of the platter was a silver and gold cake shaped like a turtle. Then a crown of lotus flowers surrounded the turtle's head.

"Oh, that is so lovely!" I cried. "Mason, you
planned it all out, didn't you?"

"Look what's on top of the crown, Charisma,"
Mason said.

I looked down and opened my mouth in shocked.
Nestled amongst the lotus was a platinum diamond ring
that captured all the angles of light. It was so brilliant and
breathtaking.

Mason took the ring from the cake and went down
on one knee in front of me. "I hope this is only the
beginning," Mason said directly, "because I can't think of
any more exciting merger than that of you and I for a long
time to come. I love you with all my heart, Charisma,
more than anyone and anything in the world. I can't
imagine life without you by my side. Will you marry
me?"

I could only gasp and fan myself as tears rolled
down my cheeks. I have come to love this man for all the
right reasons. Not for greed, ambition, status, or pity; but
for love, shared values, love and pride of our families, and
respect and admiration for each other. He had become my

best friend and passionate lover; someone who I know I could start a family with and live the rest of my life with as a wonderful partner.

"Yes," I said. "I will marry you, Mason Beast."

The room applauded, and Mason swept me up in his arms, kissing me and beaming with happiness.

He set me down and raised a toast, "Now begin our Happily Ever After…"

***

Hope you enjoyed Beautiful Girl! If you did, please feel free to spread that enjoyment to others by recommending this book to friends and family.

And if you are so inclined and kind, by reviewing this book.

Beautiful Girl: Modern Beauty and Beast (Happy Ever After Standalone Novel Series)

Authors like myself rely on the support and kindness of readers of our books through sharing the buy links, writing reviews, and spreading the word about this book; in order for us to continue writing and providing you with stories you'll love.

Thank you for all your Support!

And for your Generosity, we are providing you with a Gift of 3 books at:

http://bit.ly/2dXz8Sd

CASTING NEWS for BEAUTIFUL GIRL!

BEAUTIFUL GIRL is going to be made into a tv mini-series with a premiere date in 2017!!!

We are casting for:

CHARISMA CHU – a drop-dead gorgeous Eurasian (Half-Asian, half-Anglo) young woman between the ages of 18-30 to play a 22 year old. Must be comfortable with graphic kissing and nudity. Beautiful Girl will be for a TV-Mature Audience.

MASON BEAST – Handsome suave billionaire-type young man in his mid-20s. Dark hair and Green eyes. Charming, sensitive, and gives off an aura like Christian Grey. Must be sexy and in shape with 6-pack abs. Comfortable with graphic kissing and nudity. Beautiful Girl will be for a TV-Mature Audience.

CALLUM BEAST – Handsome Pretty Boy underwear model type in his late 20s. Dark blonde to Brunette hair. Tall and broad-shoulders, athletic. Able to go from being a villain to being a broken and vulnerable person. Large emotional range. Must be sexy and in shape with 6-pack abs. Comfortable with nudity. Beautiful Girl will be for a TV-Mature Audience.

Send a link to your page on IMDB or website with your headshot, full-length body photo, and acting experience to:

casting@sparklesoup.com

Subject Line: Beautiful Girl